'A day in the life of a northern girl'

QUENTIN COPE

To Lorraine
With Best Wishes

Quentin

Jan 2026

MECURIAN BOOKS

COPYRIGHT & DISCLAIMER

CONTENTS

INTRODUCTION

'Em' is a simple story celebrating northern culture and in particular the North East of England, a place regularly receiving attention from a national press ... for all the wrong reasons. This snapshot of life in a Northern town describes the struggle and stress of one strikingly beautiful young girl coping with the chaotic emotional needs of an alcoholic mother, a younger brother on a fast track route to an early custodial sentence and an oversexed boss with wandering hands showing little signs of repentance any time soon.

This captivating narrative is written in twenty four chapters, one for each hour of one single day in the life of Emily Macklam. Much of the conversation offers the reader a true flavour of interaction between well crafted characters and sharp minded personalities. It will hopefully make you smile in many places and perhaps leave you thoughtful in others.

'Em' is a celebration of a great and unique sense of humour to be found in a magnificent place called Hartlepool. But its focus is just twenty four hours in the life of one gutsy young woman; someone determined to bury her past, cope adequately with the present and pursue a determined plan for a future.

It's not the waking ... It's the rising ...

Chapter One
6.00 am

The booming in her head arrived as something akin to an over recorded soundtrack from some vintage Doctor Who. But why was she hearing it now, at the very moment Justin Bieber had agreed to get his kit off? He actually stood in front of her, the image appearing closer and closer, separating itself from the emerging apparition; the top half of a shimmering, sweat laden, tanned torso now in temptingly full focus with other previously blurred and distant features gradually clearing. A pair of smooth skinned, finely developed hands dropped to waist level, beginning to tug suggestively at the belt on a pair of fashionably threadbare jeans.

The resonating, fiercely unwelcome intrusion came to her louder and louder, blanking out all pleasurable thoughts, forcing the image of one tantalisingly fit looking Justin to retreat back into distant darkness. She begged, she implored; she would have shed tears if necessary. She cajoled and coaxed but nothing would tempt him back and as the vibrating, rhythmic noise became truly unbearable ... she woke.

The insufferable cacophony had stopped; or had it somehow transformed into a slow, steady bleep from a bedside alarm clock giving out a warning that would only hold value if she was to look at the digits filling the backlit display. 'Six o'clock' they shouted as she turned her head and through half opened eyes guided a seemingly disconnected limb in the direction of the offending timepiece, feeling for the device that would put an end to her continuing semi conscious discomfort. She felt exhausted and the day was only just beginning. Had Justin Bieber played his part? She felt down between her legs, expecting a dampness that wasn't there. It looked like Justin was possibly not all he was cracked up to be. Shit ... time to get up!

Emily Macklam had a plan. Some would more than likely call it a 'routine' but for her it was 'a plan' ... a plan to get her mother into some semblance of preparedness for the day ahead and her troublesome sixteen year old brother Thomas off to school. Whether he actually attended school or not, she didn't really know, and neither did she care. The 'plan' was to surmount all obstacles that morning and get herself to work on-time, with a smile on her face and a willingness to labour the obligatory eight hours that would see out this particular Friday, releasing her for whatever delights may lay ahead over the weekend.

Emily lived in one bedroom of a three bed roomed property owned by the local council, an address the Macklam family now called home. The room was more than a near square area of containment with views of green fields and grazing horses available from the single opening window. It was also her stronghold, protected by a door fitted with a stout lock and bolt offering some level of protection from the sometimes confusing and intimidating place outside of it. This then was her particular world, a place she sat and slept; a place she smiled in now and again and a place she more than often cried in during some particularly unbearable days and even more frequent depressingly lonely nights.

The drinking of the rent money on a regular basis had forced a move on the Macklam family from a perfectly adequate three bed flat, located in the middle of town, to this particular property, situated in one of the old mining villages. However, despite the inconvenience of now living outside of Hartlepool, the move had provided Emily with a small degree of hope. Perhaps being relocated ten or so miles away from her drunken, sponging and equally addicted town drinking buddies would allow Emily to work harder with her mother; get her off the booze and back into the real world of hard graft, feral children and unclaimed responsibilities.

It was probably too much to hope for. Instead of plucking Eva Macklam from a circle of dedicated alcoholics, Emily found there were just as many willing to join her mother in all day drinking sessions outside of town as there were in it.

The shower struggled, as it had done for some weeks now, the mixer tap refusing to function as it should and promises by the council to fix the problem leaving the matter still unresolved. Her mother found it difficult to keep herself sober enough to hold a decent conversation with the tenant help line, and so her few nearly unintelligible complaints on the subject were left to fall on purposely deaf ears. Council rules did not allow a nineteen year old daughter, whose name was not on the lease, to make any sort of complaint whatsoever which meant that when the winter came Emily would have to find a suitable way of solving the problem.

Life in the North East had recently been

something of a perilous existence for Emily Macklam. 'Em' was the product of a father, Jack, who finished his very last shift at the Easington Colliery during the dark days of 1994; the last pit to close in County Durham. He walked away with a small bonus of sorts and the perfectly propagated seeds of a lung disease that would eventually take his life, days before Emily's fourth birthday.

When Jack Macklam passed on, to a hopefully better and less pain racked world, he left behind him a grieving wife, someone who lacked the strength of character she had witnessed in others over the years to lift her head and carry on regardless. Her life revolved around her man and her children were regarded by her as the by-product of their life together. When Jack selfishly left her, any obvious love she may have had for her two children went with him. Her new life as an alcoholic began at the wake and for someone who rarely tackled anything stronger than a small glass of Ginger Wine, a full bottle of scotch whiskey was bound to leave her near to comatose, sprawled without inhibition across the front room sofa as the last pitying family friend quietly departed.

Emily didn't remember much about the event itself; the burial and the attending flock of people who were complete strangers to her, all dressed in black. She could however remember the violent coughing fits, the blackened foul smelling sputum; the breathlessness, the sad wide eyes from which tears fell regularly; not tears for himself but tears for his family condemned to live in various shades of poverty and distress without his guiding hand for possibly years to come.

One thing Emily knew for sure was that her

mother had taken Jack's passing particularly badly. Many would say Jack and Eva together could never be regarded as an obviously loving couple, but they were of solid Geordie stock, protective of each other and left lost in a wilderness of kind but substance free words spouted by politicians who told them there would be work aplenty when the mines finally closed. Even for fit men this was at best an untruth and for someone such as Jack, with a rapidly deteriorating set of lungs, choked with fine coal dust, this was a major deception.

Target time for the shower, quick form makeup and room tidy had been set for a work day at no more than twenty five minutes. Emily checked her watch. Two minutes late.

'Thomas!' she shouted: 'Get ye'sel up ... get ye' arse out'a bed ... quick like. Ah'm runnin' late ..!'

It would be the only warning to Thomas. Her priority was now to wake her Mum and introduce her to another day, another period in her life she would pass through in various stages of real consciousness; some stages where words from her mouth would be firmly linked to the words being generated by her brain and others where Emily knew there would be no connection whatsoever.

The room stank, the unwelcome aroma nearly overpowering her as she pushed open the bedroom door. Eva Macklam had been sick again during the night; yet more time consuming work to do in order to clean it all up. The vomit and the smell was not the problem, she was used to it. For Emily it was the sheer physical effort involved in levering her fifty eight year old overweight mother up from the floor and onto the bed; a dead weight, an uncooperative body. She shouted Thomas again; she would need his strength. He hated it. Hated entering the stench, the enduring mess, the sickness and soiled clothing but he knew his sister needed help and if he was to avoid the threat of a clip round the ear that day, he had better attend the angry and demanding voice.

'Ah'm na' comin' in there if she's bin' sick agin' like. Ah'll throw up myself ye' know. Honest Sis, Ah'll just throw up man. A'h canna' do this every bloody day ...'

'Just ye' get ye' backside in here an' help me Thomas ... ye' know A'h can't do it on me own!'

'We should have somebody to help us Em' Thomas gave out as he moved to join forces with his sister in the necessary heaving and levering of the uncooperative body.

'She's ye' mother lad ... ye' must never forget that. When ye' Da died, he took a big chunk o' her wi' him ... an there's no gettin' away from that bonnie lad. It's the cards we bin dealt ... an' so we just have te' bloody well play em' ... d'ya understand Thomas ... d'ya really understand lad?'

Thomas muttered a few incomprehensible words under his breath and threw himself into the final heave.

Between the two of them the problem was eventually solved leaving Emily and Thomas's mother finally propped up in bed. Emily began stripping her night clothing whilst Thomas ran to the bathroom to return with a bowl of hot soapy water, some cloths and a towel. He then headed for the bathroom once more to prepare himself for yet another day of shouting, screaming, bullying and what some at Manner Academy would label as simply outright mischief.

'Come on Ma' ... fe God's sake, please try an' help a little' Emily pleaded as she finished drying her mother down. Eva's eyes were open now and her lips moving continually, forming some strange shapes, none of which resulted in any word that Emily was able to recognise. She consulted her watch. Ten minutes to seven. Back on schedule but feeling physically spent.

Getting her mother into the shower had always required a good understanding of logistics and the science of levers required to move and lift weights. But it was now an element of her daily plan, one that had become a well practised routine and there was little doubt Eva Macklam tried her best to be co-operative and some days the result was better than others. Today was thankfully a good day with assistance only required to provide a generous rub down with a bath towel, help with underwear and finally the donning of a simple grey tracksuit, the recognisable uniform of most drunks inhabiting her particular world.

Finally pushing her mother's feet into a pair of well worn slippers she kissed her on the forehead and for the very first time that day, the saucer like brown eyes caught hers as a single tear fell.

'A'h know Ma ... A'h know ...' she said comfortingly.

For a few brief seconds Emily Macklam felt a near overpowering need to hug her mother; give her comfort, let her know that her only daughter loved her and wanted her to get better because she knew as well as anyone her drinking was simply an illness; an illness that could be cured if a whole band of people could just join forces and come together to change all their lives forever. But Emily had refused and would continue to refuse all social services approaches to become her mother's registered carer. She had a future; she wanted a future but she would not have one if she shut her life down by becoming a paid carer. This is what the social services wanted of course, just to push the whole damn problem of her dysfunctional family onto a nineteen year old girl and all for a few measly pounds a week.

Emily cupped her mother's chilled hands as another silent tear fell.

'But A'h have te' face the day as well ye' know, so let's take it on together eh?'

The first smile confirmed it; hopefully there would be many more that day driven by something resembling a calming emotion rather than fuelled simply by alcohol.

'A'h ye' comin' down fe' breakfast like?' Emily asked.

Eve nodded her head. Another half smile.

'Well ye' take ye' time Ma and Ah'll get some toast an' eggs on the go. Is that al' right?

'Yes Em ... that'l be fine Pet ...'

The first words of the day and it wasn't quite yet seven o'clock.

Chapter Two
7.00 am

The insistence that everyone in the house took breakfast on board had been one of Emily's early rules. There was naturally a good reason for it. Emily quickly learned during her early years of being an unpaid but dutiful attendant to her mother, and a father to her brother, that if her two charges only ate when they felt like it then Emily would be spending more than half her life in the damned kitchen.

Her way of ensuring her mother and brother had at least one intake of useful food each day was to provide some protein and carbohydrates at breakfast and then, after that, whatever they each did to top-up with calories would be down to them. Thomas had school dinners to look forward to, when he actually turned up at school of course, and her mother had a supply of microwave cook-able mini-dinners in the freezer, requiring little or no effort to put on a plate. Today was toast and boiled egg day and by ten past seven, Thomas had already arrived downstairs waiting for his two eggs to reach the four minute mark. As the hands on the kitchen clock moved round to indicate the final seconds had passed, Emily lifted out the eggs, cupping them and placing them on a plate to join two slices of crisp brown buttered toast.

'There ye' go Tom ...' she indicated.

'Thanks Em ...' Thomas offered as he reached for the nearby tea spoon to crack the tops of the eggs.

'What ye' doin' at school today?'

'Nout!'

'Nout ... how on earth can ye' be doing nout lad? When ye' Ma comes down, she'll be askin' ye' ... and ye'd better have a more useful bloody answer than that!'

'Well ... it's just school Sis, the same damn thing happens every day. What do ye' want me te' say?'

'A'h want ye' te tell ye' Ma ye'll be doing Maths or somethin' like that and ... err ... like ... err ... ye' like it and ye're good at it. A'h don't want ye' to tell her ye'll be bunking off again or probably brought home by the bloody polis now do A'h?'

'OK' Thomas muttered as he moved his attention from one egg to the other.

Would Thomas actually be attending school at all that day? It may well have been part of his sister's plan ... but it was not part of his! He was not supposed to have a mobile phone, but he did. He had already been on it earlier that morning, contacting his somewhat older 'mates' in nearby Middlesbrough. A day of risky excitement had already been arranged; events calculated to replace the normal boring activities on offer at Manner Academy.

A noise could be heard on the stairs. Their mother would shortly be making an appearance.

After finishing one egg and half of the other, one slice of toast and two cups of tea, Eve Macklam sat back in her chair at the kitchen table and proceeded to break wind. Tom caught Emily's eye leaving both with a quickly fabricated masking look suppressing the inevitable reaction. It happened regularly with each event purposely and comically ignored by their mother. However both Thomas and Emily had never gotten used to it and every time it occurred, in company or not, they had a hard time restraining themselves from bursting into near uncontrollable laughter.

'Can A'h have ye' toast Ma?' Thomas asked.

'Of course ye' can dear' came the smiling reply: 'help ye'sel luv and if ye' want some more ... Ah'm sure Em will make ye' some ...'

'There is no more Ma. There is no more damned bread for toast. This is the last of it. Tomorrow Ah'll have to go to Liddle ... so Ah'll need some money'

At the mention of the word 'money' Eva Macklam's eyes glazed over, her head making a quick movement to avoid Emily's interrogative gaze. Eve knew her daughter had hidden all the money in the house; her money, miner's pension money; benefits money ... her bloody money! So ...what was wrong with treating herself now and again with a wee drink of Whiskey and a long refreshing glass of White Lightning Cider?

Emily finished her last piece of toast with a sigh knowing well as soon as she left the house her mother would literally pull the place apart to find 'her' money. Searching for new and innovative ways to conceal cash in the house had become more and more difficult. However, it was a necessary exercise resulting in a little drama needing to be played out on a more or less weekly basis. If she had her way she would spend every single penny of it on booze inviting all her drunken 'friends' to the house, joining her in sessions that sometimes went on round the clock.

She had tried taking all the money she needed for 'housekeeping' and bill paying out of the house with her when she went to work but her mother had called the police saying she had been robbed. The police were naturally full of regret, knowing well the situation her and her mother were in, but their advice was firm, even though the stupidity of it was plain to see. In the presence of the twenty year old embarrassingly tongue tied family social worker they advised Emily she could not take money her mother claimed out of the house without her permission, so she simply hid it every day. Sometimes it worked ... and sometimes it didn't.

'What'll ye' be doin' at school today Tom?' His mother asked.

Tom and Emily exchanged meaningful glances.

'Ah'll be doin' me numbers today Ma' Tom replied through a rueful smile.

'Aye ... you're good at ye' numbers eh lad?'

'Top of the class Ma ...!'

'That's good then ... ye'll need ye' numbers if ye' don't want te' gi' down the pit lad'

'There's no damn pit's left Ma. Didn't ye' know ... there's no bloody pit's left! Everyone's on benefits, wandering round al damned day wi' bugger-all te' do ... didn't ye' know that Ma?'

'That's enough Tom!' stated Emily firmly.

His mother looked confused, but said nothing. The subject needed to be changed quickly or else Eve Macklam would be retreating into one of her dangerously reflective moods; one that would require perhaps a sip or two of whiskey to oil the brain cells in a thought process seeking confirmation the pits in County Durham had long gone ... and taken Jack Macklam with them. It was far too early for her mother to start on the hard stuff.

Emily's withering look silenced Thomas immediately.

'Tom's doin' right well at school are'nt ye' lad?' she said quickly, looking for some co-operation from her brother.

'Aye ... well, Ah've bin goin' for quite a few weeks now wi'out a break like. In't that right our Sis?' he confirmed.

'Oh ... that's right Tom. That's absolutely right!'

'Except one day last week ... and a day the week before when the damned polis dragged ye' home' muttered Eve across a half empty tea cup.

Emily caught it.

'No Ma ... the polis brought Tom home 'cause he w'a bein' attacked by a bunch of crazy's in town. Honest Ma ... wasn't that right Tom? There's a bunch of crazy's got it in for 'im. They're all drunks Ma ... bloody drunks and its ye' bring the bastards round here Ma. Now they know Tom and when they see 'im out they keep attacking 'im ... trying to get him to steal money from ye' Ma ... aint that right Tom?'

'Yes Em ... aye that's right enough like!'

Emily's mother did not answer; did not want to further the conversation. She knew they were lying. Young Thomas was a criminal ... she knew that well enough and Emily spent most of her damn time covering up for him. He needed a bloody good whipping ... that's what he needed and if his Da had been alive, he would have collected a few bruises by now, bruises he would remember every time he dipped his hands into her money. It was all a conspiracy of course but not such a clever one that it could slide too easily past Eva Macklam.

They would both be out the house soon and then she could start the search. If she was successful, Liddle would be doing her service in the booze department a long time before her daughter got there. If she found enough, she could probably have a few buddies round.

Both Emily and Thomas knew the look accompanying the silence and both hoped beyond hope the hiding place for today would remain undiscovered.

The clock on the kitchen wall showed five minutes to eight. It was ten minutes fast and purposely kept so as a visible form of encouragement in getting Thomas through the door in the morning and down to the bus stop. Since their father had died and various miner related government payments had stopped coming through the door, the Macklam family had been forced to move from the town of Hartlepool to more affordable council provided village accommodation, some several miles outside of it. So now life for the Macklam's was ruled by the efficiency, or otherwise, of the local bus companies ... and that left much to be desired.

The last bus to get Thomas to school and Emily to work on time would leave their nearest stop at eight o'clock. If it was late, then both would be late. For Thomas, school started at eight forty-five and he had a short walk from the bus station to the school gates. If he was late it would incur lots of verbal from teachers and yet another black mark against his name. For Emily, if she was late for work it would mean a five minute 'chat' with the store manager and searching looks from the rest of the staff.

'Ye'd better get a shift on lad' offered Emily walking through to the hall way and reaching for her coat.

'Kiss ye' Ma goodbye!' she shouted, opening the front door, checking her pockets for the essential purse, mobile phone and set of keys. Tom followed seconds later, slamming the front door behind him.

The violent noise, although not unexpected from

this particular sixteen year old teenager leaving the house, made Eva Macklan start. She checked the kitchen clock. Now she was alone ... and the search could begin.

******

Spring in County Durham and Cleveland had been good that year but now it was surely about to be replaced with some warmer days heralding the onset of summer. Emily had dressed in a lightweight jacket that morning although the temperature could well be described as 'chilly'. Doris Crowe and Wendy Roberts, regular commuters on the eight o'clock, greeted Emily with the normal conversation opener in that part of the world; the weather.

'Mornin' Em ... bloody cold this morning like; brass monkey weather comin' soon no doubt'

Wendy sniggered at the brass monkey reference with both her and Doris ignoring Thomas completely.

'Mornin' you two' Emily replied, pulling her lightweight jacket against her a little tighter at the first mention of brass monkey's that summer. All three smiled leaving Thomas occupying himself, as he normally did, with rhythmically kicking at a ground level Perspex shelter infill panel as part of a plan in his mind to eventually break it.

The dark blue shape of the number 49 grew as the bus lumbered nearer. Emily checked her watch. Three minutes to eight. She would be at work on time today and Thomas would have no excuse for not attending school at the allotted time of eight forty-five ... bliss! No threatening phone calls from a school manager to contend with and no pitying looks from the staff at Pettigrew's Hardware and Building Supplies to bear in rebellious silence throughout the morning.

'It's Friday ...' Emily shouted toward Doris as the bus pulled up and came to a gentle stop.

'It sure is Pet' Doris replied: 'We'll be spending an hour or two down the club like, te'night ... won't we Wendy?'

'Aye we will Dor. There's a great new act on; like them Chipperdales or somethin', ye' know the ones wi' muscles an' a sun tan. Are ye' comin' wi' us Em ... our men are out at football ... so we'll have a great night on our own ... won't we Dor?'

'We will that!'

'Not tonight ladies. As long as the bloody house is not stacked wi' drunks when I get home ... I'll be out me'sel like and getting the awld' dancing shoes polished up'

'Good on ye' girl' Doris confirmed: 'As long as ye' Ma don't find the hidden treasure ... Eh?'

All three women laughed as the bus doors closed with a reassuring hiss.

Chapter Three
8.00 am

Conversation on the 49 gathered pace as at each bus stop more ladies heading for work in town piled on board. Despite several teenagers also taking up the journey none of them spoke to Thomas, or more accurately purposely avoided talking to him. This had started when Thomas first went to secondary school and Emily initially queried the situation. Perhaps for some mystifyingly and purposely opaque reason, Thomas was being ostracised by his peers; possibly because of who he was, what he did or what he said. It was a worrying situation and when questioned about it by Emily, the boy just shrugged his shoulders.

It wasn't until a year or so later she began to understand why no one spoke to him; they were all frightened to death of him. Thomas was a scrapper ... and a damned mean one at that. He had a close circle of friends at school, or more accurately described by the police as 'accomplices' who joined him on his various 'outings' into town to smoke cigarettes, practice a bit of shop lifting and on the odd occasion rip the ignition out of an old car and go joy riding along the coast. Emily didn't worry about him anymore. If the lad was planning on spending half his damned life in prison, then so be it.

The raucous and sometimes embarrassingly honest banter between the ladies had become the regular prelude to a working day destined to be spent behind a till at Asda's, in a cleaning crew at the Premier Inn, on a packing line at some food factory or other or being a public facing stores assistant at Pettigrew's Hardware.

'So ... are ye' comin' te' the club wi' us tonite Em? Doris shouted: 'Our Joan who saw em last week in Middlesbrough reckons one o' these Chiperdales had a one eyed trouser snake that's a right bobby dazzla ... and so bloody gross it kept fallin' outa' his draws ... an' winkin' at her like!'

Doris' words caused screams of laughter from the rest of the girls.

'No Dor, A'h couldn't handle anything like that. The last one that winked at me fell out o' a bag o' willicks!'

Emily's reference to a bag of 'winkles' now had everyone on the bus in fits.

'Ye canna' get a bairn from a bag o' willicks Em' shouted Wendy.

'Aye, and ye canna' get a day's work from a one eyed snake ... so give me the bloody willicks any time ..!'

'So what ye' doing tonite then Em?' asked a giggling Ange who worked on a factory packing line: 'If A'h looked like ye girl, I'd be shoein' me'sel into the tightest thing A'h could carry in me handbag and get searching for that one eyed snake ... show the little doylem what a good night's work looks like...!'

The laughter continued.

'Na Ange, A'h always end up wi' a wazzock out te' get maaahrtal ... so Ah'll just keep on dancin' an' rustle up Justin Beiber later when I'm in me scratcha like'

'Well Em, Ah'll tell ye' there's one good thing about bein' married. It puts an' end te' all this Justin Beiber crap. Ye' can talk about sex an' stuff, wi' ye' partner wi'out embarrassment Pet. Our Tony said the other day, when we're havin' sex, next Sunday morning like, why don't we swap positions, just for a change? A'h said that's a crackin idea Pet ... you stand in front o' the ironing board like ... an' I'll stand in front of the Tele ... an' fart!'

******

By eight thirty the bus had begun to disgorge all its passengers with the young blushing driver fending off comments from the ladies on his looks and tattoos along with some speculation as to the size and capabilities of a certain snake like object. Doris worked hard at being the worst, tempting him with offers of a night of carnal bliss ... as long as it was Tuesday ... the night her Kev played darts.

Emily shouted a quick goodbye to Thomas who shifted off at no particular speed leaving her focused on getting to Pettigrew's before nine. Ange walked with her half the way.

'Ye've got trouble wi' that lad o' yours Em' Ange offered as they exited the bus station at a brisk walking pace.

'Aye, A'h know that Ange, but Ah'm not bloody well sacrificing me life te' look after him, the lazy little bastard. Ah'm getting the hell outa' here as soon as A'h bloody well can Pet. Ah've been saving up like ... an Ah've only a couple o months to go for me BTEC level 3 certificate. Once A'h get that, Ah'm off ... and Ah'll take great pleasure in tellin' that snotty nosed southern twat of a manager at Pettigrew's to stick his job as far up his arse as he can get it!'

'Well ... that sounds bloody great Em. Where'll ye' go like ... I mean, will ye' be round here or ...'

'Ah'm off to London Ange. One o' them big

stores like Selfridge or Harrods or somethin' ... A'h know A'h can do it Ange ... A'h damn well know A'h can do it!'

'Ye've no problem there Pet. Lookin' like ye' do, there's na' need for any bloody certificate; those barmy London sods will be fightin' over themselves te' give ye' more than a bloody job when ye' get down there lass!'

They both laughed out loud, perhaps a little nervously to camouflage the less than obvious signs of envy from Ange and the tiniest level of trepidation from Emily.

Time to part company.

'Bye Em' shouted Ange as she walked away: '... an' don't forget if ye' want te' join us tonite like ... just gi' us a ring!'

******

Pettigrew's Hardware was part of a small family managed chain of businesses based mainly in the north and midlands, with a head office in Watford. The reason for the head office being so remote from the actual businesses was the man who ran it all. Jonothan Pettigrew, son of the founder, preferred the southern lifestyle with his socialite wife, privately educated children and his multi-million pound house set amongst the hallowed green and well manicured pastures of sunny Hertfordshire.

As a result, although all the retail outlets were staffed by locals, each business was necessarily managed by someone hand-picked by Jonothan; someone whose retail talents had usually been discovered lurking not too far from his local golf course. Rumours amongst Pettigrew staff revealed that all the managers were complete 'twats' and if the one where Emily worked was anything to go by, the rumours were all correct.

She walked through the rear staff entrance at ten minutes to nine and clocked on. The team at Emily's Pettigrew's averaged about thirty in all including staff required to work the small timber and building supplies yard attached to the side of the hardware business. Staff came ... and went and turnover of individuals had become a problem. Emily had been at Pettigrew's for nearly two years and it took that long just to know where everything was on the damned shelves.

By most measures, Emily Macklam was a striking looking young lady; tall at over five feet nine inches without heels, a well rounded slim figure, short cropped and perfectly shaped dark brown, bouncy hair framing a clear skinned, lightly tanned face, describable easily as naturally photogenic. Only five other women worked at Emily's Pettigrew's with two of them customer facing and the remaining three working in the upstairs accounts department. Emily was still a trainee on a basic wage rate of just under six pounds an hour. When she finished her BTEC, planned for before the end of the year, she would be a recognised and qualified member of staff and could expect to see a staggering rise in income of approximately twenty pence an hour.

So, for Emily, although life in general was shit, she could see light at the end of her particular tunnel. She had a natural flair for her work, always looked the very best she could with the meagre resources available to her and brimmed with confidence in everything she undertook.

Emily was nothing if not focused on learning,

having definitely discovered much during her couple of years of customer facing experience in the largest hardware and building supplies business in town. She had learnt how to take a compliment, how to brush off meaningful advances from lads who fancied their chances and how to hold her own in the game of shop floor politics. There was only one particular stumbling block to coming out of her training with a clean sheet and the much cherished BTEC certificate and that was someone named ... Peter Lewis.

Peter Lewis was the appointed manager at Emily's particular Pettigrew's and, to his way of thinking, master of all he surveyed. In fact an employee vote on the shop floor and in the yard would describe him as simply a mid thirties, pinstripe suited idiot. Unfortunately, from Emily's point of view, he was not only an idiot but a particularly annoying idiot with wandering eyes and barely restrained searching hands.

He appeared as if by magic in the locker room as Emily donned her dark blue overall and pinned her name badge to the front lapel.

'Hi Emily ... pleased to see you're on time this morning' he muttered through a thin, forced smile.

He moved forward until he was now only a few tempting inches away from her.

'Probably had a restless night then ...' he offered as part statement and part question.

'Naah Peter. Unfortunately A'h wa' woken up durin' the night wi' a terrible nightmare ... an' it wa' like one o' them horror films ye' know ... like the ones where the virgin maiden get's all sorts of things done te' her'

She leaned forward, her firm breasts now only millimetres away from his perfectly pressed suit jacket. There were signs of perspiration.

'Oh ... and did you know this person who was doing all these ... all these ... err ... terrible things to you Em?'

'Oh A'h did Peter ... it wa' you Pet ... it wa' you alright, an' that's why I woke up ... it made me feel bloody sick man!'

The damp looking store manager made a short whimpering sound and then half jumped back a step, searching for words through Emily's mocking laughter. He could find none ... as usual, turning and making a quick exit from the locker room.

Would this be the only one on one contact she would have today with the normally office bound manager? She doubted it. He would find some excuse or other to suddenly appear right beside her when no one was about. He had an instinct for it, a depressingly accurate instinct for it. At some point, before she actually left the employ of Pettigrew's, she would ensure there was some form of memorable physical contact between them, but not the kind he would be expecting ... or hoping for!

She checked the wall clock. Two minutes to nine; time to open up. As she walked through the store shouting 'good mornings' to all the unseen staff lurking between the aisles, one bantering male voice shouted back: 'Pistol Pete not able to detain ye' this morning then Pet?'

'Na ... Howay man, divvin be daft. That knacka? Giz a bag o' crisps'

Laughter and the odd snigger followed Emily to the front of the shop, customers peering through the sliding glass doors; guaranteed to be male, mostly self employed, unhappily married and in a hurry with many shouting comments too rude to be repeated in front of the wife.

Another day was about to begin for Emily Macklam; another day of positive earning power and one more step nearer her goal. As long as she could keep the lecherous Peter Lewis at arm's length and finish her shift without some long drawn out confrontation with an unhappy customer, then she would be able to breathe a particular sigh of relief knowing the possible hedonistic pleasures of a Friday night on the town with the 'girls' would be that much closer.

Hitting the security key pad and pushing the power button, the doors slid open and a small crowd of waiting punters rushed past Emily, eager to get their hands on some essential item or other required to finish their 'Friday' job ... and get paid. For her customers it was the end of another week's work and time a well earned financial reckoning. For Emily Macklam another day at her particular coal face had just begun.

Chapter Four
9.00 am

By nine fifteen Emily had served three of the early regulars with a trained smile and just the right amount of banter. Her colleagues on the floor had managed to sort out the rest, leaving the morning rush completely satisfied and the store temporarily empty of customers.

Billy Saunders had managed to survive the fags, the foundry smoke and the failure of many whippets on the race track to reach his late fifties and looked as if he had suffered several years more than that. With a bad back limiting most lifting activities, Billy would solicit help, when required, with a polite request. However fit he actually was, he had been made the senior customer advisor on the floor and held a father-like soft spot for Emily. Early morning duties included shelf stacking and they would often work together; him doing the remote stock entries and her doing the physical work, filling the shelves. He had concerns for Emily knowing her background and home situation. Her mother was an alcoholic wreck and her young brother, unless he turned his life around very quickly, could only be considered a major jail sentence simply waiting to happen.

'So ... Friday night Em. Ye'll be out tonite then?'

'Aye, A'h will that Billy' Emily confirmed.

'Don't ye' get inta ne' trouble now ye' hear!' came the caring reply.

'Ne' bother Billy. I'm in'ta toon for a drink like an' a bit o' dancing ... an' if some good lookin' lad takes me fancy, he may get lucky!'

Billy chuckled quietly to himself as he pressed another button on his remote stock updater. The input time showed nine twenty five.

Kylie, one of the sixteen year old floor trainees, approached the happily working team, interrupting the shelf stacking. The look said it all. No personal mobile phones were allowed on the floor; company rules. However, messages could be left on the business landline for employees as long as such messages related to a fairly well defined level of urgency.

'There's a phone for ye' in the office Em!' advised Kylie. Emily and Billy exchanged glances.

'Let me guess' sighed Emily: 'It's that bloody cow from Tom's school again ...!'

'Aye that's right Pet ...' confirmed Kylie.

'You go and I'll finish this' advised a concerned Billy Saunders.

'Thanks Billy ... Ah'll try not te' be long like ...'

The office was a purposely uninviting place inhabited by superior beings obviously affected by their drab surroundings and as a result appeared to the rest of the staff as mostly lacking a sense of humour. Peter Lewis' glass panelled office, commonly referred to as the 'goldfish bowl', occupied the rear with the late forty something attention seeking, senior accountant Harriet Pearson working a station next to the only door through to the office space. It was obvious she was madly in love with the young Mr Lewis, although being nearly half a generation older her chances of any physical connection remained slim. However, that did not stop her trying and a bet was on with all the yard workers.

Other desks filled the space to the front with Jane Witham, a sixty year old, sour faced general clerk fielding all enquiries that may have somehow made their way up to office level. The phone on her desk lay off the hook and as Emily entered the room, the black faced clerk indicated the hand held instrument and waved it in her direction.

Emily picked it up, took a deep breath and said ... 'Hello ...?'

'Is that Emily Macklam?'

'Aye ... it is'

'This is Edna Stevenson from the Manner Academy. I have to tell you that your brother, Thomas, has not appeared today ... is there any reason for that?'

'Why ye' askin' me like? Ah'm not his bloody bodyguard. Why don't ye' ring me Mam?'

'Your mother is not answering the number we have for her here, and ...'

'That's cause it changes every bloody day like, cause she keeps on giving her phones awa' te' her bloody drunken friends man. All A'h can tell ye' is he wa on the bus wi' me this morning and I saw him off the bus in town. That's all A'h can tell ye' an' that's the truth of it!'

'I'm afraid that's not good enough Emily' replied a stern toned school office manager.

'So, what d'ye want me te' do about it? Ah'm his bloody sister ... not his damned keeper!'

'You have two fines outstanding already ... you know that. If he's not back in school by lunch break, then they'll be another fine; your mother will go to court and if the fines are not paid then someone is likely to go to prison!'

'Well Pet, it bloody well won't be me. A spell

inside will do em' both good ... so fine away lass. An' by the way, what gives you the bloody right te' hassle me at work like? My boss is getting right pissed off wi' all this. Ah'm not allowed phone calls at work ... I've told ye' this before but ye' don't seem te' want te' take any damn notice!'

The office had become silent ... every person there listening intently to what Emily had to say. When the call first arrived at her desk, sour faced Jane could simply have told a persistent Edna Stevenson staff were not allowed to take calls unrelated to company business, and that would have been the end of it ... but no. She made Emily answer the caller from Manner Academy to simply embarrass her, and in the process provide some unexpected entertainment to the rest of the office.

The smirk on the face of Jane Witham said it all as she pretended to scribble on a piece of scrap paper, ears flapping like an elephant in season. Even the over painted Harriet pushed Peter Lewis's door wide open so he too could wallow for a few entertaining minutes in Emily's misfortune. Edna Stevenson was nothing if not persistent.

'Can you not go out in your dinner break ... and see if you can find him in town?' she asked firmly.

'No ... A'h bloody well can't!' came the shrill reply: 'You've a damn cheek you have. Fancy asking me te' go lookin' for me brother just because ye bloody school has lost complete control of him. Ah'll be ringin' the social later an' tellin' em what ye've just asked me te' do. I think ye' must be gannin micey like!'

The phone went silent. A 'micey' school office manager was perhaps considering her options.

'Well, there's no more to do then Emily. I'll just

have to call the police and let them sort it out. This will go badly for the family I'm afraid and ...'

'No ... your bloody nosiness, it won't go bad fe' me ... it'll go bad for Thomas. Me Ma won't give a shit as by the time the rozzers get round home, she'll be out of it on White Lightnin. It won't go bad for me cause he's not me' bloody problem. So do ye worst lassie an' for god's sake ... stop ringing me at work man ... ye hear?'

With that, Emily slammed the phone instrument back in its cradle on Jane Witham's desk causing her to start visibly.

She looked up. All eyes rested on her; even an obviously interested Peter Lewis peered out from his goldfish bowl with the 'lovely' Harriet standing guard on the open office door.

For a second, Emily felt a demonstration of her anger at being forced to have a conversation with Miss Stevenson in front of an office full of wazzocks could justifiably be called for. However, her sensible head advised against it with only weeks to go to holding her treasured BTEC qualifications in her hand. They would be her ticket out of this damn place and all the Edna Stevenson's and Jane Witham's in it. She would simply have to bloody well grin and bear it. She turned to face the room and lifted her chin.

'What ye' all looking at like?' she shouted as every head suddenly discovered some important document to attend to on the desk in front of them. That damn Thomas was causing her pain and trouble yet again. Literally not one day had gone by in the past few months where Emily hadn't had to deal with some issue or other associated with the lad. If he was not at school, then it was a fair bet he would be out with his scumbag mates, stealing cars and joyriding ... or worse. Something needed to be done but all the so called 'authorities' wanted to do was shove the responsibility back onto Emily. It was a hopeless situation and every time she received a phone call from the snotty nosed Edna Stevenson, she became more and more determined to get out of her situation, make a clean break, a fresh start in a new place where opportunity rather than hopelessness greeted her every day.

Back on the floor Emily looked for Billy. At least there was one sensible person she could talk to at Pettigrew's.

'Was it who A'h think it was?' he asked.

'Aye ... it wa that pillock of a woman Edna Stevenson'

'So, Tom not at school again Pet?'

'No Billy. The little shit has done it again. There's sod all A'h can do to control him. He just lies all the bloody time. Me Ma simply don't care Billy; there's nee talkin to her ... her bloody brain's stopped workin like. If she's found the money A'h hid last night, she'll have it all gone by the afternoon an the'll be ne scran in the dammed house'

Billy moved to put a comforting arm around his favourite sales person. She smiled up at him, fighting hard to hold back a tear. Emily would not cry today. She was stronger than that; more focused, more determined than most to make a life away from what she saw as an opportunity-less North East. Having a doylem of a brother and a stinking alcoholic mother would not stop her. She knew where she was going ... and so did Billy.

'Nee bother pet. If ye'll be short, just pop round our house. Me and the missus think the world of ye, ye know that and if ye need anything ... anything at all, we'll help ye best we can like. Ye know that ...'

At that very moment, all Emily wanted to do was cuddle up tight to Billy, spending a few trouble free, pain free seconds in a warm, protecting embrace; a fathers hug, a rock in the stormy sea of a cruel life, a gamblers hand as it had been dealt to her; life for a northern girl.

She gently pulled away to avoid the release of bulbous tears that welled and sought escape as her emotions levelled once more at Billy's comforting words.

'Thanks Billy but hopefully she'll only find some of it, the rest A'h have in me pocket ... an' I can buy some basics wi' that tomorro'

Billy smiled.

'Come on then girlie ... let's finish this damned stacking an then it might be time for a cup o' tea like!'

'Ho'way man ... that sounds greet!'

Chapter Five
10.00 am

Friday could be a busy day at Pettigrew's especially if the weather was fine. By ten o'clock Emily had finished a quick stock check with Billy and served several customers, most of which were local builders and tradesmen who enjoyed account facilities and some good discounts at the town's leading private hardware store. She knew many of the regular customers, young and old. Often one of the younger 'hopefuls' would make a beeline for her with some nebulas query or other in order to express their undying devotion if 'Em' would only spend some quality time with them in the back of a draughty van, accompanied by some brain numbing head banging music and several cans of brown ale.

One young lad in particular, a plumber from Peterlee, would come into Pettigrew's every Friday to settle his account. It could easily have been done on-line of course, as did just about everyone else, but John wanted the excuse to capture some time with Emily and if she was not free when he entered the shop, he would wander around until she was.

'Mornin Em' he offered as he slid up to till counter number four.

'Mornin Scraggy' she replied.

She knew his actual name was John, but everyone seemed to call him by his nickname of 'Scraggy', something linked to a Pokemon character seemingly, the logic of which floated way above Emily's head. She wasn't interested in being in the back of a draughty van with him, whatever his name was ... and he knew it.

'So ... what's me account like Pet? A'h did'ne bring me statement wi' me so A'h hope Ah've enough cash to pay 'an hopefully there'll be some left over ... so we can go out for a quick drink te'nite like'

Scraggy put on his best boyish smile.

'Ye'r a right gadgie you Scrag. A'hve told ye' twenty times, there'll be no courtin' between me an' you if ye' had all the damn money in the world and a willy like a Tesco cucumber!'

'Aw, that's setting the bar a bit high Em. Them Tesco cucumbers are canny like, but would ye settle for something from the bargin' veggie section at Aldi's?'

'Now come on man, Ah hav'ne all day te' gas wi' you. Ah've got ye' bill here so dee' as ye' tel't and pay up quick like ... Ah've got other things te' do the'day!'

'Aw, c'mon Em ... A'h just wanna know what A'h have te' aspire to like ... so tell me ... how de ye' really like ye' men ...?'

'Well done ... wi' no bloody chips! Now, pay ye' bill and sod off will ye' man ... Ah've got things te' do an' Ah've no time to stand here massaging ye' damn ego an jawin' on man'

Scraggy looked visibly hurt as he fished a plastic card from an overstuffed wallet. He handed it over and when the transaction had been completed, he turned to walk away. After a couple of steps he turned back again, his face alight with a grin from ear to ear and shouted.

'Thanks for that Em. So I'll see ye' tonite like on board me schooner moored on the Tyne. Eight thirty ... and dress as if ye' mean it pet!'

'Piss off Scraggy ... ye gannin' a bit nutty like'

Emily shouted back causing the odd ripple of laughter from those within earshot.

At quarter to eleven Billy caught Emily's eye and nodded his head in the direction of the tea room. She nodded back. Billy made a great cup of tea but to him it was something of a ritual, taking time and patience; so he headed off to begin the process. Water had to be boiled and then left to stand for some time. The cups, or in this case mugs, had to be China, not plastic and warmed with boiling water first. The tea bags required a particularly timed infusion and milk must only be added when the black unsweetened tea had rested for a minute. Finally, sugar could be added if required and low and behold, the perfect cuppa would appear ready for the first tasting.

Billy also provided biscuits; chocolate digestives normally but occasionally he would lash out with some jammy dodgers. Today the special treat appeared on Billy's personal white china tea plate, complete with press patterned paper doyley.

They both sipped at their tea in silence. Only two others on the floor took their break at the same time as Billy and Emily. Both males in their late twenties, they normally sat together studying their mobile phones in complete silence at the far end of the long narrow ground floor storage area used mainly as a tea room.

Billy opened up the conversation.

'A'h' ye' OK Pet?' he asked: 'Ye look a bit dark round the eyes like. Has that cow from Tom's school upset ye'?'

'No Billy. A'h can handle her. Anyway, in a month o' two's time she'll have no cause te' ring me. Our Thomas will be leavin' that damned school but then

A'h think me problems will really start. He doesn't give a shit right now about anything and every time I look in his face, A'h can't see nothin' of me Da there ... ye know, it's sort of frightening really, I just canna' make a connection wi' him like!'

'Ye mother's got te' step up te' the bloody plate Pet ... take some responsibility and tell the young tosser the truth about his'sel. She has to do it Em and let ye' off the hook. I've offered before an' Aha'll do it again Pet; if ye' want me to pop round and have a firm word wi' her like ... then I'm happy to ...'

Emily interrupted, reaching for his hand; a comforting move designed to emphasize a particular message.

'Thanks Billy, but she has te' do it on her own. She has te' admit that me Da ... is not his Da. It's something I'll never forgive her for, expecting us to believe he wa' up te' making her pregnant in the condition he were in. He could hardly make his bloody legs stand up let alone his willy and after all these years ... for her to still stick to her soddin' story makes me want te' give her a damned good smackin' like!'

'Do ye' think if she told him Em, gave him the full details and the name of his father ... he would calm down; the rebellion would end?'

'A'h just don't know Billy. He's far too big for me te' handle now. Although he's still a kid at sixteen he's in a man's body and a pretty damn big one at that. Aye, an he's a canny wee bugger. He knows how to twock a car wi' all his smoggie mates an although he signed up for college after the end of the summer term, everybody knows he'll never be there ... an A'h suppose Ah'll end up gettin' all the shite for it like!'

Billy remained thoughtful and concerned. He

knew the pressure his best salesperson had to bear, not least of which were the wandering hands and lustful looks of the boss at Pettigrew's. Emily needed her BTEC certificates and as she was being sponsored by the company, the mean willed manager, Lewis, commonly referred to by all the staff as 'that southern twat', had the power keep her in a job ... or sack her, something that would put an end to her immediate ambitions, forcing her to start again working for her final certificate with someone else.

'Ah'm just so pissed off wi' me Ma Billy. Whether she finds the housekeeping A'h hid or not, she'll be off her bloody head by three o'clock; she'll find the money from somewhere or her mucky bloody drunken mates'll gi' it te' her an' te tell the truth half her problem is guilt over the way she tret' me Da. As far as she thinks, it were her that killed him not the bloody mine ... an' that may not be far from the truth of course. A'h were too young to remember what the hell was going on, but one thing's for sure, unless she unloads all her shit, she'll never stop the booze like ... never Billy ... never!'

She gave his hand an extra squeeze.

'What if he gets put away? From what ye've told me he's on the last o' three strikes an' if he gets caught again they'll put him in a young offenders ... an' once in there his card'll be marked for good Pet. I can talk wi' ye' Ma, but a stranger like me telling him the truth of his parentage could possibly push him over the edge. It will have to come preferably from his Mother ... or perhaps from you'

'Well it aint' comin' from me Billy ... that's for damn sure, an' Ah'm not covering for him nay more with the rozers like. He's out again today an what's the bettin' he'll be down Middlesbrough way by now joy riding in some poor buggers pride and joy. When they bring him home in a bloody box then perhaps me Ma'll start to tak' notice like. It'll be a bit late then won't it Billy ... it'll be a bit bloody late then won't it?'

Emily glanced at her watch.

'Time to go me mate. Back to the bloody grindstone'

As they both entered the floor the be-suited 'southern twat' hovered by till number two. He purposely checked his watch. Billy spotted him and checked his. Two minutes to eleven. No chance of a bollocking there then with just two minutes to go before the morning break could be considered officially ended. Perhaps he was building up to something. Billy and Emily exchanged glances. She had a mischevious air about her.

The dissolute eyes of Peter Lewis locked onto Emily. Billy had seen the look many times before and had been logging all such contact between the two of them for over a year. Emily half waved in Lewis's direction adding in a forced, broad smile.

'Are ye' OK there Mr Lewis?' she shouted: 'D'ye need me te' ring somethin' up for ye' ... or d'ye want me te' book out some tools for ye' to try at home like?'

'Don't damn well do that Em; you're just winding him up and one day he's goin te' bite back ... hard! I know he lusts after ye' like, but try an' keep it all at a distance ... at least until ye' get ye' hands on them damn certificates'

'Aye, ye' right Billy, as usual. Ah'll try and make an effort, but he does piss me off, an' one o' these days A'hm goin' te' have to sock him like!'

They both laughed out loud as a reddening Peter

Lewis, the well dressed 'southern twat', marched quickly away to climb the short stairway up to the office, a place of security for him; a place he was respected and even loved by the likes of the devoted Harriet Pearson.

On the shop floor the word was getting round fast and this was the signal for the banter to start; words of wisdom from between the aisle-ways and behind the display boards.

'A'h heard the southern twat sent ye' a valentines card this year Em, and he put the address of Aldi's car park on it!

'Aw shut ye cackle man' Emily batted back. She knew the voice. His name was Greg, the company joker.

'OK Em ... tell me the difference between a bus full o' southern twats and a hedgehog?'

'A hedgehog has al' the pricks on the outside man ... now shut ye' chatter an' get on wi' ye' work!'

Even Billy had to laugh at that one.

Chapter Six
11.00 am

Customer complaints and the handling of them had become a speciality of Emily Macklam. She had rarely been intimidated by bullying individuals, especially those who felt their concerns were not being dealt with seriously by being put in front of an ordinary member of floor staff ... and a rather young and possibly inexperienced female at that. The object of the exercise for Pettigrew staff however was to keep the complainant on the floor of the store and not have to refer him or her upstairs to 'the office' where he or she would have to face an unhappy Mr. Lewis.

This was of course not Pettigrew policy; it was in fact 'Lewis' policy and one designed to keep him away from the 'conflict zone'. The manager, for some unknown reason, found himself incapable of handling angry or even slightly upset customers and a request for 'my money back' would send him into a tailspin. His world was enclosed in glass and guarded very efficiently by the devoted and much praised Harriet Pearson. He wanted nothing else but to remain barricaded in his crystal fortress for eight and a half hours a day, playing with figures, adjusting and readjusting stock levels and making choices as to which new arrival in the power-tools department he should take home next for trial and evaluation.

Peter Lewis was not a customer facing manager. He generally hated customers. They could interfere with his working day; the more aggressive ones sometimes pushed into committing the greatest sin of all by turning the ever protective Harriet to tears. No, one thing was for sure, Peter Lewis ... or 'lily livered Lewis' as the girls called him, was not fit for front line duty and must be protected from the customers at every stage of an ongoing complaint process.

Arthur Greening operated his own landscaping company. He was not seen as a particularly regular customer at Pettigrew's but he did pop in now and again if looking for items he couldn't readily lay his hands on elsewhere. This had been the case a week previously when trying to source a cubic metre or two of pebbles to dress some terraces on a fairly substantial project he was finishing for a regional house builder.

He had ordered from Pettigrew's ninety bags of fifteen to thirty millimetre sized polished black ornamental stones. They had been delivered to site and some bags had been opened and pebbles spread. The main contractor had rejected the product on the basis of colour. He wanted a much lighter, greyer tone and so Mr Greening would like to have the load he had ordered ... and paid for, collected from site and his money back.

To him, the matter was a simple one. He had opened several bags and started to lay them before they were rejected so had scooped up as many pebbles as he could by hand and placed them back in the opened bags. He would be happy to pay for a collection by Pettigrew's but he would like all the money back for the purchase.

Emily greeted Mr Greening's problem with a beaming smile, an approach designed to give her time to establish a quick measure of the man. Billy Saunders hovered behind a display panel, listening into the conversation and poised ready to assist. This could be a tricky issue to resolve and the last thing Lewis the manager would want plonked on his immaculately polished and problem free executive desk.

'So ... Mister Greening, sorry but perhaps A'h missed ye' first name like ...?'

'It's Arthur ... Arthur Greening' the customer confirmed.

'Well Arthur, let's see if Ah've got this right then. Now ye've been into the shop like an' picked out some stones te' have delivered te' ye' worksite. Is that correct?'

'Yes it is'

'So we delivered em ... an' when your customer saw em, he rejected em because they were the wrong colour. Am I right so far Arthur?'

'Yes. So far one hundred per cent correct' muttered Greening.

'However, now some o' the bags ha' been opened like and ye've had to shove the stones back in te' the bags ... is that correct Arthur?'

'Yes it is' repeated a now impatient looking landscaper.

'So, how many bags are opened Arthur?'

'There's eight in all ...'

'Well Arthur, I feel sure the stones ye' have put back in the bags are clean and all there like, but unfortunately our head office has a strict policy on returns and even if A'h wa' te' get down on me knees an' beg, they would'na accept an opened bagged item back for refund. Can ye' see that Arthur, they just would'na accept them bags back!'

Her look had gradually turned to one of wide eyed sympathy as she leaned forward toward Arthur, gradually decreasing the few inches separating them ... and most importantly, maintaining eye contact.

'That's no good to me lass. I want the full price back; there's nothing wrong with the stones and my foreman assures me they are all there, either in the bags or on the pallets'

'A'h can see ye' point there Arthur, A'h mean it's not your fault ye' had to open the bags. Will the site manager not let ye' use em' somewhere else like?'

'No he bloody well will not. Now let me see the manager. I haven't got all day to spend standing here jawin with you ... I've got a business to run!'

'Well Ah'm sure ye' feel a bit frustrated right now Arthur, an' A'h can understand that ... an' on behalf of the company A'h can only apologise to ye' like, so let's see if A'h can come up wi' something that'll help to solve the problem'

'The only thing that'll solve my problem will be you giving me my bloody money ... right now ... so I can get back to work!'

'Well Arthur, Ah'll get the manager for ye' in a minute like, but first A'h just want te' see if there's a way round the problem and we can get ye' on ye' way'

Arthur Greening remained silent. He was a Yorkshire-man, dower in his ways and used to calling a spade a spade ... not a shovel. This was why he normally dealt with the big boys of the industry where a situation like this would have been handled with a 'no problem' response once the supplier checked the amount of money going through the Greening account. They were not worried by a few opened bags of damn stones, they needed volume and turnover and a customer who spent more than ten thousand pounds a month was a customer needing to be looked after, and as part of that process they would be more than happy to swallow the small costs involved.

This very attractive young lady was obviously trying her best to help him but all he wanted was his money back and to get on his way. His business was based in Leeds but he often carried out work for main contractors in the North East … if the price was right. He had only patronised Pettigrew's on this one occasion because they had the shade of stones he thought his client wanted. Having several pallets of rejected stone taking up space in his storage yard was not what he had planned for.

The young lady … Emily the name badge said, was busy playing with the computer.

'Err … Look Miss, can you just get me the manager and then we can sort this out, I really have to go and …'

'My word Arthur' Emily interrupted: 'It looks as if ye' don't have an account wi' us like. Now that's just silly. Whoever took ye' order for the stones should have told ye' about our discounts for account holders like'

'I don't really need an account here; I rarely use you in this part of the world. I work all over the country and have accounts with MKM and Travis Perkins … nationwide. I only came to you because you had the damn black stones and …'

'Now then Arthur, A'hve been doin' a bit of calculatin' Pet and if ye'd have had an account when ye ordered the stones, ye would have gotten a twelve and a half percent regular customers discount … so …'

Arthur looked up … taking notice. The word discount had been mentioned.

'Nobody told me about discounts' he said firmly.

'Well then Arthur, I think we have a way round this wi'out getting managers involved an' all that palava like'

'OK ... tell me what you've got ... as long as it doesn't take all day'

'Right then Arthur! It looks to me as if you've paid full price for ninety bags, thirty kilos each at thirty five pounds per bag ... including delivery. Is that right Pet?'

'Yes' confirmed Arthur.

'Well that makes a total of three thousand one hundred an' fifty pounds. Is that right Arthur?'

The landscaper consulted his invoice, confirming the price was correct.

'Now eight spoiled bags comes te' two hundred and eighty pounds but a standard account holders discount of twelve and a half percent would come to ... three hundred and ninety three pound and seventy five pence'

Emily's face lit up forcing a smile from Arthur.

'So Arthur, if I backdate your account facility to the date of this invoice, your discount will cover the eight spoiled bags and put you in credit to the amount of one hundred and thirteen pounds and seventy five pence. How about that then Pet?'

Arthur Greening couldn't quite get his head round it but what this attractive and intelligent salesperson seemed to be telling him had apparently become the solution to the problem. He nodded his head as some form of acceptance, allowing Emily to continue. Billy, still concealed behind the display panel, smiled from ear to ear ... 'the girl done good!'

'Well now, if we take sixty pound o' that left over money to cover the collection costs, then you will leave here today with the stones returned and an account in credit to the tune of fifty three pounds and seventy five pence. Are ye able to accept that Arthur?'

'Well ... I suppose so ...' confirmed the thoughtful, still slightly confused but generally relieved customer.

'Good. Then gi' me a minute te' get the paperwork sorted Arthur and Ah'll give ye' a receipt an' a collection date. Once we have the bags back here an' inspected like, we'll send ye' a cheque for the balance'

Five minutes later a satisfied Arthur Greening exited the premises of Pettigrew's Hardware and Building Supplies still trying to work out how he had come into the store prepared to do battle in returning some opened bags and have to pay for a site collection when in fact he had walked out of the store with the whole order returned, the collection paid for and an account in credit to the tune of over fifty pounds.

'Everything all right wi' that customer Em?' Billy enquired as he wandered past counter number two. Emily finished jotting something in the back of a till receipt and looked up.

'Oh aye Billy. Nice man that Mr Greening. He's opened an account wi' us now so hopefully we'll be seein' a lot more of him'

'Need me for anything?' he queried.

'Aye ... well if ye could just countersign this account opening like ... it looks as if it should ha' been done last week when he first came in te place an order Billy ... but I think the paperwork must a' got lost ... !'

She smiled the wonderfully captivating 'Em' smile as she handed him the till receipt.

'Aye Em ... it looks as if someone's been a bit sloppy like. Anyway, thankfully it's done now ... and it looks like we can safely say we've claimed another regular customer Pet'

'A reet bobby dazzla Billy' Emily confirmed with a

smile in her voice, heading towards the stairs leading up to the office on a mission to arrange Mr Greening's collection.

'Those bloody southern softies won't know what the hell has hit em' when she gets down there. She'll wipe the bloody floor wi' all of em' ... her an' her damn BTEC certificates' Billy muttered happily to himself.

Chapter Seven
12.00 am

It had been a busy day so far. Emily consulted her watch confirming the time shown on the big store clock; a few minutes past twelve. Her lunch-break would be due at a quarter past and she would need to seek out Billy to let him know when she was going. The sandwich van, owned and operated by Molly, usually arrived in Pettigrew's substantial attached car park at around twelve and stayed until about twenty five past, depending upon the weather ... and the amount of trade. The near spotless travelling kitchen was amusingly titled 'The Canny Scran Van' and the parking spot at Pettigrew's served several local businesses on the small trading estate.

Molly perhaps looked a little older but she was only twenty two, a tough cookie, married with two kids and an out of work 'useless bastard' of a husband ... at least that's how she normally described him. She had started the successful business from scratch and desperately wanted to put another van on the road with Emily Macklam behind the wheel. Molly was ambitious and desperately looking to generate an income that would free her from her current council house existence lorded over by out-of-work Bobby, the person she was unfortunately married to.

Emily and Molly were two of a kind where ambition was concerned and they had talked about joining forces and putting another van to work often. The issue right now was that Emily only held a learner's driving licence but no matter what possible fortunes lay behind a partnership in 'The Canny Scran Van' franchise, she remained very much focused on her proposed new life in London.

At twenty past, Emily appeared at the end of the remaining small queue of punters, many of whom had waited patiently for Molly to arrive since before twelve.

'Mornin Molly' she shouted to the busy but well organised entrepreneur.

'Morning Em' came the quick reply, not looking up from her current culinary construction.

'Busy day?'

'Aye, it has been that Pet. Ah'm out o' burgers like. Them bloody shits at the building site round the back o' ye' here et' the soddin lot. I'll have te' gan back yem' after servin' yous' like and pick up some more stock. Ye' see Em, if ye' was wi' me like, we could cover so much more ground an' carry much more stock an ...'

'Don't go there Molly for Christ's sake. Just get me a damn chicken an' avocado roll an' a cup o' tee' ... an' quick like ... Ah'm bloody starving man!'

With freshly made roll in one hand and cup of tea in the other, Emily voted to sit outside for her half hour lunch break. One or two benches, fitted as part of a small landscaped area at the top end of the car park, had been originally designed to showcase to customers some options for paving stones, decorative gravels and small timber structures. However, the seating had been taken over by staff as a place to take breaks as opposed to the windowless slightly smelly locker cum store cum break room.

As Emily was about to sit down she heard a car horn. It bleeped a couple of times. She looked around her and immediately her heart sank. A blue Ford

Fiesta could just be seen at the bottom of the parking area and someone was sitting inside it. Emily knew who it was. The car belonged to WPC Shelly Beecham and it looked as if she wanted a conversation.

Finishing the last of her completely satisfying chicken and avocado roll, Emily reluctantly levered herself up from the wooden bench and with remaining tea in hand made her way toward the blue Fiesta.

Sitting in the front with Shelly, Emily knew what was coming. Shelly felt sorry for the young, but tough and extremely attractive nineteen year old, saddled with a disastrous home life and trapped between a drunken, scheming mother and a dangerously out of control brother. However, she had a job to do and as part of the Cleveland Anti-Social Behaviour Team she had been tasked with keeping offending youth's out of prison. Receiving attention from Shelly and her colleagues was considered the last chance saloon for persistent young offenders and particularly for Thomas Macklam, the end of the road was definitely in sight.

'So Emily ... you probably know why I'm here?'

'A'h do that Pet' Emily replied grumpily.

'Young Thomas is now sitting in the Hartlepool nick with two regular, older offenders, from Middlesbrough'

Shelly waited for the words to take effect. The expression on Emily's face remained unchanged. 'Here we go again!'

'Do you want to know what he's in for?'

No reply.

'He ... and his two accomplices, fished a set of keys from a house for a nearly new Range Rover, stole it from the drive of the house ... and then went joy riding in it ... round Teeside!'

Emily remained wordless. She had heard it all before. It used to be twenty year old Ford's ... but now Thomas had seemingly graduated to considerably more expensive Range Rover's.

Shelly sighed heavily as a sign of irritation that Emily had so far remained unresponsive.

'They were chased by police for over an hour through back-roads, several mining villages and then along the A19 and north up the A1 causing a major disruption to traffic. Eventually they crashed just outside Shotton Colliery ... and one of the lads is seriously injured'

'Which lad ... is it our Thomas?' Emily asked; concern now showing on her face.

'No. It was the lad who was driving. The other lad and your Thomas got away with scratches and bruises. The Range Rover is a write off and they've clipped a few parked cars on their morning joyride as well as damaging two police cars, leaving what some have called a trail of bloody disaster!'

'Soo ... he's al' reet' then?

'Yes ... he's all right but you really have a problem with him Emily ...'

'Naa Miss bloody Shelly; it's ye' wi' the problem like. A'hm just his sister and not even his full sister de' ye' know! So don't ye' come round here badgerin' me at work like an' tellin' me about him. De ye understand?'

'So what do you want us to do? He's in the nick right now and he'll be damn well staying there unless you come down and go some sort of surety for him. He's only sixteen for Christ's sake and something has to be done about changing his ways or else the next time it'll be a young offenders and then, only a couple of years down the line it'll be full on, grown up prison. Do you understand the importance of what I'm saying Emily?'

A beleaguered Emily Macklam knew the game. One of the few emotions capable of being successfully transmitted down a phone line ... or across the front seats of a blue Ford Fiesta was GUILT!' Shelly Beecham wanted to make Emily feel guilty about her family situation; push her into becoming the 'responsible adult' in the case of Thomas and fully paid up, full time carer for her alcoholic wreck of a mother. During the past twelve months, Emily had battled this slightly sinister, self serving approach from both the police and the social services ... and she was having none of it!

'Why the hell are ye' putting pressure on me like? Why don't ye' get round te' me yem and drag me' Ma down' te' the bloody nick; get her te' do all ye' bloody surety and things. I'm only a girl like an A'h should'ne have to deal wi' things like this. So, I'll tell ye' how A'h see it Shelly. Stop pissin' about an' put the little shit in prison ... and then take that lazy, useless drunken cow an' put her in the cell next te' im' like ... d'ya get the picture now lass?'

A minute of ponderous silence and a long, drawn out sigh from the detective constable indicated her frustration at not being able to get through to the only hope left for her to make some connection with Emily's delinquent half brother. She knew the story of Thomas as it had been told to her by Emily and also knew of, and had listened to, many insistent denials from Eva Macklam concerning the fatherhood of her son. There would be no DNA testing; no long meaningful conversations with twenty year old trainee psychologists ... there would be nothing other than a flat refusal to discuss the matter of Thomas' birth and more importantly, his conception. As Emily had reiterated many times, Jack Macklam in two thousand and three couldn't raise himself out of his chair unaided let alone have functional sex with his wife ... someone who had slept in a separate room for several months due to the disturbing, constant coughing and gagging of her terminally ill husband.

Drunk or sober, Eva Macklam refused to discuss the heritage of her son for whatever reason. During her rare, fully lucid moments, she would receive and understand the messages being delivered by her daughter concerning Thomas and his increasingly out of control behaviour. Was there some deep secret attached to any detailed revelation relating to his birth, something that perhaps must never be discussed?

When Thomas arrived, Jack never questioned the matter; never commented on it to friends and simply took the young male child into his arms and smiled; the only thing to make him smile during those final dark days.

Emily checked her watch. He dinner break was slowly ebbing away.

'What are we going to do with Thomas ... Emily?' asked Constable Shelly Beecham in a quiet, purposely soothing tone. The last thing she wanted was to have to constantly hassle this lovely young girl, someone boasting a tough, defiant exterior but designed to protect what she was sure would be a gentle and caring personality beneath.

'Look, since me' Da died and we had te' move out o' town ... because we couldn't afford the bloody rent, plonkin us down in the middle of a pissing little village with no way te' get around like has cut the boy off from his school friends an' all the things they do together. A'h know how bloody hard it is; A'h had te' do it mesel' like'

'But you didn't resort to stealing cars Em!'

'I know ... but it's different for him. You've tried and I've tried to talk wi' the council and get us moved back inte' town wi' the same rent we have in the village ... but they useless bastards won't hear of it. So, here we are!'

'But what do we do to get him on the straight and narrow?'

'Ah've told ye' before; get me damn Ma on the straight an' narrow; stop her bloody drinkin' and hangin' around wi' all them shaggin' local alcoholics. Ye' have te' get her clean and then get her involved. That's what everyone should be focused on ... NOT ME! Get the social services, the council, the police and the bloody charities who reckon they care about what direction his life is goin' in ... an' bloody well do somethin' about it. That's what needs to happen Shelly ... that's what really needs to happen. De ye understand lass?'

'I do Emily ... unfortunately I do and that's why I'm here bothering you right now'

'Well, don't bother te' bother me any more ... right? I have me life an me Ma and brother have theirs ... an they will have to manage theirs as I have to manage mine ... an that's the end of it!'

'Well perhaps you'd better not expect him home tonight Em'

'I don't expect him home any bloody night Holly!'

With that final word she exited the car and strode up the car park toward the store. She would be late back and that bastard Lewis would be watching no doubt.

As she walked in, Billy caught her eye; a damp eye with Emily determined not to let the impending tear fall or acknowledge its presence by wiping it with the sleeve of her overall.

'Everything all right Em' a concerned Billy asked.

'Aye, everything's OK Billy ... just that bloody Holly woman tryin' to create even more shit in me life like'

'Thomas again?' he queried.

'Aye ... bloody Thomas again' she confirmed.

'You take another ten minutes off if ye' like ... I'll cover for ye'

'No thanks Billy, that's very kind of ye', but I just want te' get back te' work and forget about it all'

Although Emily Macklam showed only her granite exterior to members of the Cleveland Police Force and Constable Shelly Beecham in particular, she did have feelings for her brother. No matter how he had arrived in the world and what his genetic makeup would prove to be, he had lived in the same house as part of the same family as Emily for all of his life and therefore she was entitled to feel for him as a brother. Although life in the Macklam household had always been, and would continue to be, a struggle after the breadwinner, her father, had died, there had been many happy moments and as a young boy Thomas had been a joy to be with. But now his life was heading down the toilet and much as she wanted to help him, if she did, they would all quickly shovel their 'shite' on her and then her life would be buggered. The council, the police and all the bloody do-gooders would, without fail figure out some way to dump all their responsibilities for the lad and then point the finger when it all went tit's up.

Emily was having none of it. She was on her way to London and anyone who didn't understand that ... had not been listening. Thomas thought his big sister would be around forever; someone to come home to when things didn't go as expected, someone to keep his mother clean, fed and watered, someone to sort out all the damn house maintenance problems with an uncaring and uncooperative council ... but he was wrong!

The impending tear looked as if it might win the battle for freedom and so Emily quickly excused herself from Billy's company and headed toward the staff toilets. No one at Pettigrew's had ever seen Emily shed a tear before for any reason and today was not to be the first. Perhaps a damn good cry would clear a mind clogged with talk about her drunken Ma, her delinquent brother and all the piss poor social services characters who wandered in and out of their lives with nothing to offer other than yet one more bloody fifty page form to fill in.

Chapter Eight
1.00 pm

With makeup repaired and no detectable sign of damp eyes, Emily took a deep breath and pushed on the toilet door leading out to the staff locker room. He was there ... just inches away. Her eyes searched the room quickly. Except for him it was empty. The wall clock showed the time; ten minutes past one. He was so close she could feel the heat of his ashtray breath.

Peter Lewis was a smoker, a heavy smoker and in the twenty first century, this was not a popular habit. Only one other person at Pettigrew's smoked and he was a fork lift driver in the yard. None of Emily's friends smoked and for a non-smoker, the rancid fumes emitting from the half open orifice of the store manager gave away his unwanted presence.

One arm stretched out to the wall, limiting her options for freedom. This particular pose however did provide an obvious and tempting opportunity. One well placed kick upward at that particular moment into his sensitive and unprotected area would do it; would put him on the floor rolling in agony. She knew how to do it; she had practiced the technique once before in an effort to cool the overheated carnal desires of a gangly semi drunken youth, someone who felt he was owed a little more than a goodnight peck on the cheek. It had taken place at the back of the Seaman's Rest pub on a chilly winter's night some months previously and she was as confident in her ability to hit the target now as she was then.

They were both roughly the same height; eyes set at the same level, unspoken messages passing between them ... Peter Lewis hoping it would possibly be his lucky day and Emily Macklam determined that it most certainly would not be.

'Friday night Em' he said in a thick voice. Was it a statement or a question?

'Aye Peter ... it's Friday al'right ... an' that would make tonight Friday night like!'

'So, what are you doing tonight then ...?' he persisted, offering out his best panty-dropping grin.

'Same as your wife pet!' she replied blank faced, providing nothing more than what could only be described as a stony expression. Her interrogator coloured; a sign of dampness now showing on a blushing forehead.

The unexpected response had stumped the manager for a brief moment.

Lewis did not come on to Emily all that heavily very often, perhaps once every six months or so, but when he did he was a complete pain in the arse. The sexist banter was OK with her; she could hold her own in most situations, especially those involving over sexed and under satisfied men of any just about age or era. However, today Peter Lewis appeared to be overstepping the mark, so she thought she might stoke the fire just a little bit.

'The missus not letting ye' have it lately Peter ... pressures building up like and now ye'll be lookin' for a cum bucket ... someone to dump ye' load in'te; ye' know quick and hard like ... in the ladies toilets! Is that what ye'll be after Peter, a blow job in the toilets ... very upmarket Pet, very southern like?'

The face on the suddenly less than confident predator suffused crimson as Emily spat the words at him; contemptuous words un-weighted with emotion, her knee now slightly raised, spring like, ready to release upward with all her energy if he made one single move to grab her and push her back into the toilet area.

'I really don't know what you've got against me Em. I try so hard to be your friend ... a real friend as well as your manager ... and all I get is bloody abuse'

'Well, ye' have it there pet; it's the something that's the hard bit A'h don't like. For God's sake man, ye' have a lovely young wife an' bairn at home; ye' should be satisfied wi' that like and not chasing after innocent young girls like me!'

She smiled thinly, underlining the sarcasm of the delivery.

The ensuing silence indicated a thought process of sorts could possibly be in progress. Would he now just walk away after receiving two forcefully delivered put-downs; simple but effective words of rejection from this unbelievably attractive northern lass, or would he change his approach in an attempt to appear slightly more subtle?

'Joan is away this weekend at her mother's, in fact she's just rung to tell me she's on her way. So I'm just at a bit of a loose end tonight, that's all. I'd be quite happy to take you out for a drink somewhere and perhaps we could discuss your upcoming BTEC final assessment ... you know ... just discuss it and tie up any loose ends'

'A'h didn't naa there were any loose ends Peter. A'h mean, what loose ends could ye' be reffering to; what could there possibly be like?'

His hand left the wall and he moved an inch or so to the right; a change in body language; a change in approach.

'Well, you've passed all your paperwork tests Em ... with flying colours I believe and really what will take you to the top of the class will be the final practical assessment ... and a concluding interview with ... me!'

'A'h know that pet an' so does just about every bloody worker here at Pettigrew's. If ye' cock up me damned BTEC, I promise I'll do for ye' an' ye' won't like it Peter ... ye' damn well won't like it!'

Peter Lewis's eyes darted from side to side nervously. Had he miscalculated; gone too far? Emily's face tightened into an expressionless mask. This poncy southern bastard had never been so directly obvious before.

'No Em, you have me wrong. I'm not saying you will get anything but a great review from me ... honestly! I'm just saying you've learnt a lot here at Pettigrew's and before I sign off on your qualifications, I just thought it would be a good idea if we spent a hour or so ... away from the job ... to just have a chat about ... about ... well, about how far you've come and what your future might look like ... but do it in a relaxed, social environment'

'Oh ... well that's absolutely great Pet. If we're all goin' te' have a social night out like ... to celebrate me getting me BTEC ... an' you're paying, then I'm sure a lot of the staff would love to come. Ah'll go an' tell em' now like. Are we still talkin' tonight or maybe another night when ye' wife can come too Peter?'

His face turned pale and twisted into something resembling a bulldog chewing a wasp. He was left desperately searching for new, more effective words. Too late! The locker room door leading directly to the floor opened and in walked Billy. Immediately suspicious, he asked straight away 'what was going on?'

Lewis turned his head sharply and instinctively moved a step back from Emily.

'Sorry Billy ... what did you say?' asked the manager in a nervous voice, a tone or two higher than normal.

'I said ... what is going on here? Are you alright Pet?'

'Aye, A'h am that Billy. Me and Mr Lewis was just discussing the party he was going to throw for all the staff like when A'h get me BTEC certificate. Isn't that right Peter?' Emily asked through a smile struggling hard not to become laughter.

'Well I ...'

'Well nothing Pet. Peter is so damn generous to his staff like. Isn't that so Billy? An' he wants to make it a right occasion an' bring his wife along. Isn't that right Peter?' she continued.

A look of bitterness crept into the face of Peter Lewis. He felt cornered and like all rats in a similar position should now be considered dangerous.

'OK. That's enough of all this rubbish. It's time you were back on the floor Emily ... and you Billy need to tell your staff this bloody locker room is a mess and someone should be allocated to clean it up ... and I don't mean later either!'

With that, a mumbling and obviously distressed Peter Lewis headed out of the locker room and forcefully closed the door behind him.

'Well, what was that all about Em?' Billy questioned.

'Oh ... just the normal heavy come-on from the southern twat who says his wife's gone away for the weekend like, an' A'h think he wa' lookin' for me to sort of fill in for her ...'

'I'll punch his bloody lights out if he carries on like this' stated a concerned Billy Saunders: 'Ye' shouldn't have to deal with that bastard like this. If there's any more of it A'h want ye' to make an official complaint. We'll all back ye' here and then perhaps we can get rid of the bloody tosser for good.

'Leave it Billy. It's only a few weeks now and once A'h get me BTEC Ah'll be regarded as senior staff and then Ah'll damn well sort him out ... me own way pet ... don't worry!'

'But ye' don't have to put up wi' it Em. There are laws an' things supposed to protect young girls from this kind of bloody harassment and everybody on the floor will witness for ye'. He's just a complete asshole and A'h don't know if anyone's told ye' like but he's now pushing himself on te' young Kylie. She not as tough as you Em, by anybody's standards, an' Ah'd never forgive me'sel if something wa' te' happen te her. Ah'm tellin' ye', he's got te' bloody well go ... and as soon as ye' get ye' certificates Em, then we can ...'

Emily Macklam cut Billy off.

'Howay' man ... don't ye' fret nee' more about him. He'll get what's comin' ... have nee' fear like!'

Back on the floor a few heads turned as Billy and Emily exited the locker room; the untidy locker room. They had generally sussed out what had been going on when their manager Lewis had emerged from it, red faced, sweaty and obviously angry, slamming the door hard behind him.

The shop was busy. There were queues at two tills and Emily headed for till station number three; time to put the Lewis event behind her. Billy gave out one of his encouraging smiles as he headed off to help a customer carry an awkward length of drainage pipe.

In the office, a raging Peter Lewis shut himself way in his goldfish bowl with a worried Harriet Pearson shuffling papers on her desk, glancing across at the distressed manager every few seconds. When he had calmed down a little, Harriet would gently tap on Lewis's door, enter and offer to make him a cup of tea.

He turned his head sharply and caught her eye. Everyone in the open plan office was looking, but not looking as if they were looking. The trick was simply training, and sour faced Jane Witham was the best at it.

Lewis beckoned toward Harriet who took a quick scan of the office before entering the glass edifice that was home to her young and some would say quite handsome manager. He indicated she was to sit at one of the chairs fronting his oversize desk.

'What's the matter Peter?' she asked.

Although Harriet was from the North East, born and bred, she had worked hard over the years to completely bury any indication of a Geordie accent. She hated it; did not want to be identified with it and had invented a back story to her life when questioned in company. It had something to do being born in London; parents in the armed forces; lots of travel and education at a good boarding school near Bristol. Nobody questioned it mainly because nobody cared and so 'Lady Harriet', as the staff had nicknamed her, swanned her way through the daily mire at Pettigrew's having confidence that with time and patience, she would eventually 'have her man' and the young Peter Lewis would experience the night of his life once she had managed to capture him behind a locked bedroom door.

Right now 'her man' looked unhappy and no

doubt that cheeky damn slip of a girl Emily Macklam would be at the heart of the matter somewhere. He looked up at her wondering whether or not to tell her about the incident; Emily's rudeness to him ... someone she should be looking up to not being bloody rude to ... someone who was after all her damn manager for God's sake!

'I've just had to tell some of the staff about the state of the locker room Harriet. I think we need to send out a memo or something to all the staff. It's simply not acceptable'

She knew instinctively this was not what had caused him to be so upset.

'So who was it you had to tell Peter?'

'It was Billy ... again!' the words squeezed through tight lips.

She was pretty sure that Billy might have been involved somewhere along the line, but he was not the real problem.

'Has that cheeky young bitch Emily Macklam been causing trouble again? That whole damn family is bad Peter. I don't know why you protect her like you do. She's trouble you know ... I told you that the first time she set foot inside the place. When she gets her bloody certificates ... you should get rid of her ... do you hear me Peter ... you need to get rid of her!'

A defeated looking Peter Lewis gazed up at the face spewing out sharp edged words he barely heard. The face was not a pleasing face; a heavily made-up ageing face, distorted with anger and jealousy. However, for just one split second the thought passed through his mind that maybe Harriet might like to fill the blank space in this weekend's entertainment schedule; a blank space due to the absence of his normally attentive wife. However, it was only a thought lasting for just that split second and then it was gone, banished by a further thought that any short term carnal pleasures with the not quite so handsome and much older Harriet might herald a series of more long term problems.

Harriet caught the momentary glint in Peter's eye as his thought processes continued on and hoped that this may actually be the moment. His wife was away; that she knew. This could be her chance. Was he considering it ... was he actually considering asking?

Chapter Nine
2.00 pm

Norman (Norm) Christie was one of her mother's so called 'friends', someone who Emily would often discover sprawled over the family sofa pissed out of his brains on days when her mother had managed to find the hidden housekeeping money.

He was probably a few years younger than fifty eight year old Eva and more than likely had some sort of fumbling sex with her on regular occasions. Norman had difficulty in managing his life and suffered from some type of undiagnosed mental illness. He should have been receiving medical attention, but the system had rejected him and so as far as the NHS and social services were concerned, he more or less didn't exist. Norman Christie struck a pathetic figure with an obviously big heart and little else. However, whenever he appeared there would always be some sob story or other behind the reason and Emily Macklam was well used to it.

He had never come to the store before, for any reason. When Eva had money then he preferred the comfort of Emily's front room to drink and smoke his life away, alongside his willing provider, rather than venture out into the cold, hard world of standing up straight and being polite to people. However, today he actually was standing up straight and from the tone of his opening words also making an effort to be polite.

'Have ye' got a wee minute Em?' came the question, the words delivered with difficulty.

'What are ye' doing here Norm. You're drunk ... as usual an' we don't sell Gin or White Lightnin in here ye' know. A'h think ye've been given wrong directions Pet!'

She quickly scanned the immediate area. The place was busy. She needed to get this obvious drunk, with a certain following aroma, out of the store.

'Come wi' me Norm' she instructed taking him firmly by the back of his jacket and guiding him out into the front car park and then on toward one of the benches in the small ornamental garden.

'Sit down ... and now tell me what it is ye' want. A'h don't know what on earth has brought ye' here to me place of work like, but ye' mus'nt do it again ... D'ya hear ... ye' must not come here again!'

He looked up at her, his bloodshot yellowing eyes attempting to focus; a waft of foul breath released as he opened his mouth. He searched for some suitable words, lips moving in preparation, revealing broken and stained teeth, all of which appeared to be in major need of emergency dental attention.

'Ye' Ma sent me Em. She's in a bit of a state like. The Polis ha' bin' round and they've got ye' brother locked up ...'

'A'h know that Norm. They've bin' here as well Pet, so why are ye' here like?'

He fumbled in his pockets mumbling unintelligible words.

'Have ye' got a fag Em? ... Ah've got some but A'h divvin' naa' where they are man ... I thought they were in me pocket like but ...'

'I don't smoke Norm, ye damn well know that. So stop buggering about wi' fags and stuff and tell me what ye' want ... an' then ye' must go; ye'll get me the damn sack if ye' hang around here!'

'But they've got ye' brother locked up Em an' ye' Ma want's ye' te' go get im' out like. Can ye' do that Pet ... can ye' go and sort it out like?'

'Firstly, he's not me brother, he's me half brother, an' Ah've told the rozzers what Ah'll tell you ... Ah'm not doing nothing! He can stay where he is and the boys in blue can do what the hell they like wi' him. So, if it's message carrying ye's all about now Norm, ye' can take this message back to me Ma ... Ah'm doing nothing for im' ... is that OK like?'

'But he did'ne do it Em ... ye' Ma says he did'ne do it like ...'

'Did'ne do what Norm? He was in the damn car wi' those other two bloody wazzocks. They's both a bit micey like and if our Thomas hangs round em' much longer, he'll be gannin' down' a road of self bloody destruction too!'

Norm's head fell to his chest. Had he fallen asleep? Emily nudged him.

'Wake up ye' pillock. Now A'h don't know how the hell ye' got here, but ye' gonna' have te' use shanks pony to get anywhere from Pettigrews. They won't take ye' on the bus in that damn state'

'What are we goin te' do about Thomas Em. Ye Ma is right upset like and I'll tell ye', when ye' get home, if Tom's not wi' ye', then there'll be hell to pay. She's putting em down her right now and I hate te' think what state she might be in later'

'Listen, listen to me Norm. By the time A'h get home she won't be able to bloody well stand up let alone count how many people walk through the damn door!'

Norman Christie rummaged in his jacket, pocket after pocket and eventually came up with a scrappy piece of paper with a telephone number written on it.

He shoved it toward her.

'This is the number o' the custody sergeant. Maybe ye' could just ring him and see what ye' can do like?'

'What is it about the word NO that ye' seem not te' understand Norm? Ah'm NOT goin' te' ring anybody and the little shit can stay there for the rest of his life for all I care. So that's the end of it Norm … the very end of it. Ah'm not getting him out o' trouble any more. Do ye' completely understand like? This is the end of it as far as Ah'm bloody well concerned. A'h have a life to live Norm and just 'cause you, me Ma and Thomas have all voted to throw yours down the bloody toilet, that's all your problem. So, just piss off now an' leave me alone … an if ye' come here again, Ah'll call the damn Polis and ye' can spend a night in the bloody nick yer'sel like!'

Was the drunk beside her, smelling of stale fags, booze and dry vomit, in any fit state to go anywhere? One thing was for certain, however he was to get where he was going from here, Emily would not be paying for it. No bus fare and no taxi fare. All she needed him to do was to exit the car park and then her responsibility, or even her rising feelings of guilt, would come to an end. She urged him to stand by pulling on his jacket and step by step led him to the entrance of the company property. With a small shove in the back he tottered off mumbling and muttering to himself carrying his aroma with him as he went. Emily watched the sad figure gradually retreat into the distance and when satisfied he would not be coming back, returned to her duties on the floor of Pettigrew's.

Back in the store Emily grabbed a stocking sheet

and moved into the warehouse to pick up a pallet of paint tins, pulling it back into the store with a pallet truck. Britney, a seventeen year old, recently started trainee, asked to help. She was, by nature of the title, supposed to be on a training programme but it appeared more often than not, between menial tasks, she would be left to her own devices. Billy should have been managing her better, but bless him, he found Britney a particularly difficult individual to deal with. He summed the unfortunate young lady up with his normal economy of words; 'she's thick!'

'Come on Britney, ye' can help me wi' these paint tins ... an' don't ye' go droppin' any like else ther'll be hell to pay'

'Oh thanks Em. I won't drop any ... don't worry'

Britney had a reputation for blathering but Emily had mastered the art of 'tuning out' when people were talking around her. It was a necessary coping mechanism in dealing with her mother and her entourage of barely literate alcoholics, so in passing tins to Britney the movement became mechanical as the words flowed from the trainee sales assistant's mouth.

'Of course, when A'h saw her like, A'h were angry. Bloody "Universal Credit" A'h told her ... it's a damn joke like! Me Ma can't work but 'cause Ah'm now on a wage, they've cut her money 'til she goes for an interview or something like that and we can't get te' the bottom of it like. De ye see that Em?'

'Aye' came the disinterested reply.

'So when A'h saw her, all dressed in black like, A'h thought to me'sel, she's all dressed in black like, an' I wondered if it were some kind of warnin' like, ye' know Em, like a Judge puts that black thing on is head before he tells ye' yer' having ye' head cut off ...

or somethin!'

'Yes Kylie ... Oh that last tin ... Desert Caprice ... is on the wrong shelf Pet. Just look what ye' doing eh?'

'Aye A'h will Em. So, the woman in black calls in a young man like, an' I thought to me'sel, that's funny like, she's called in a young man ... why has she called in a young man like? Well Em, this young man started talking an' A'h couldn't understand a damn word he were saying like. He were talking about me givin' up me job an' bein' a carer for me Mam. Sixty four pound a week he said, tax free he said and me Mam was noddin' her head like. D'ye know anything about this carers allowance Em?

'A'h don't know the detail of it all Kylie ...' confirmed Emily as she handed over the last of the tins on the pallet.

'Well, A'h were quite surprised like. Getting that money for doin' nothing more than A'h do now like, an' then A'h can go work in me cousins chippy at night for cash in hand like, an' that's what me Mam said, she said you could have this ... an' then work cash in hand at me cousins like!'

'Aye' offered Emily mechanically.

'So, what de ye' think Em?'

Kylie would need to ask again.

'Em, what de ye think like?'

'About what Kylie?'

'About me givin' up me job here and getting this carer's allowance thing ... it's sixty four pound a week Em, and then A'h can work cash in hand like at me cousins fish shop in the evenin's. No one's going te' know are they Pet?'

The last thing Emily wanted to do right now was offer advice to yet another indecisive teenager and knowing the social services as she did, she was pretty sure that whatever Kylie was being offered, there would definitely be a catch in it somewhere.

'Don't bloody ask me Kylie. You're on a trainin' programme arn't ye? So whoever your mentor is on this trainin' programme … go an' ask them Pet. Ah've got enough bloody problems o' me own to resolve wi'out takin' yours on board as well'

It appeared that whatever social problems existed in the North East, a place once decimated by the shutdown of major industries such as coal mining and steel production, could be handled simply by finding a teenager somewhere in the extended family and pushing them onto signing up for a carers allowance. She should of course advise Kylie to tell the social services to stick their bloody allowance and look after her mother as they should be doing. Kylie should be looking for a life, maybe a career of sorts, not picking up sixty four pound a week and then hoofing it at her cousins chip shop, hoping to Christ no one tells the authorities on her.

Kylie looked disappointed that Emily was unable to come up with anything more than she had done. It was obvious she wasn't really interested and so it appeared, neither was anyone else. Anyway, there was nothing wrong in working in a fish and chip shop; there was often some good looking fellas' getting in there!

Emily checked her watch; just past a quarter to three and only ten more minutes to go to her next break. Thank god for that.

'Oh, sorry Em' … and then Kylie started all over again!

Chapter Ten
3.00 pm

The hot cup of freshly made tea was particularly welcome; the wonderfully crumbly Biscoff biscuits even more so. David, a twenty six year old floor sales assistant, brought them. He had been at Pettigrew's since leaving school. He was a nice lad, drove an old Ford Escort with an unusual paint job and fancied the pants off Emily. He appeared as quite a shy personality when around her but dealing with customers he could be tough to the point of rudeness.

Dave, who had the same allocated afternoon break period as Emily, sat with her at one of the four small tables taking up a major part of the available space in the locker room. The biscuits had been carefully displayed for Emily's benefit on a chipped china plate positioned in the centre of the table.

'D'ye want another Em' he offered, pushing the plate an inch or two toward the person who, to him, was the most beautiful girl in the whole wide world.

'No thanks Dave' said Emily: 'A'h need to look after me figure Pet; don't want te' be getting too fat ...'

'You could never be fat Em' interrupted a smiling Dave; 'A'h think ye' have that kind o' figure that'll stay perfect for the whole of ye' life like. There are some people like that Em. A'h saw a programme about it all on tele' a week or so back ... and A'h thought about ye' like ... an' how true it was!'

The wide, boyish grin added humour to the flattering statement.

'A'h hope ye don't mind me askin' like, but is your Tom in trouble again?'

'Aye, he is ... an A'h think he'll be in a young offenders for this one. He just won't take no notice like. Me Ma's soft wi him, when she's sober enough to actually talk to anyone and as he's got bigger, he just tells me to piss off'

'Well, he's in wi a bad crowd and that's a fact. A'hve seen him out at night Em and he's often wi that team of assholes from the 'boro like ... and they're always stealin' cars an gannin' in night clubs an' causing all kinds o' bloody mayhem'

'A'h could do more Dave, but now they want to make me his sort of guardian as they've declared me Ma totally unfit due te' the bloody drink. Ah've had enough o' both o' em like. A'h just want te' get away from this bloody place an as soon as me certificates come, Ah'm on me way to London ... an' A'h aint' comin' back!'

'Ah'd come wi' ye' Em ... ye' know that don't ye'. A'h could look after ye'. That London's a bloody dark place when ye' on ye' own. We could both get a job Em an' share the costs and things. It's damned expensive livin' there Em. I've heard small flats are going for round a thousand pound a week like ... A'h mean, who on earth could afford that Em?'

Emily pushed a warm hand across the table and covered his for a brief moment.

'That's right kind of ye Dave, but A'h have to do it on me own. Ah've saved up money to get me started and wi' me certificates, Ah'm sure Ah'll get us a decent job ... so don't worry pet ... A'h think Ah'll be al'right like'

David remained quietly thoughtful for a moment.

'A penny for em?' prompted Emily.

He looked up; the pale green eyes transmitting a confusion of thoughts. Perhaps he was about to ask a question.

'How come ye never go out wi me Em?' he asked firmly.

'How come ye never asked me David!' she replied in an equally controlled tone.

He smiled through a faint look of embarrassment.

'Have I never Em?'

'No bonnie lad, ye never have. Perhaps in ye' mind ye' have like, but Ah've heard no actual words ever since Ah've known ye!'

'So ... would ye like to come out wi' me Em, out on a proper date like. A'h can take ye' te' a nice restaurant if ye like or dancing at a posh club in toon. Ye' only have to say the word'

Emily passed a reassuring hand over his once more, her expression warm and encouraging.

'Howay man, there's nothing Ah'd like more Dave, but we have te' work together and all we can ever be is friends, good friends nevertheless. D'ya see what A'h mean Pet?'

'Aye, A'h do Em, reluctantly A'h do ... but promise me when ye' get ye certificates like, we'll al' have a whopping neet out like ... before ye' go'

The depth of a smile grew; a hand squeezed fractionally tighter, a confirming re-assurance.

'A'h can promise ye' that Dave ... have ne' fear man'

With the biscuits completely devoured, a quick glance at the locker room clock advised just five minutes to go before they both had to return to the floor.

'How are things wi' the southern pillock?'

'Well, to tell ye' the truth Dave, one thing A'h will

not miss from here will be him. That Peter Lewis is a right persistent little asshole and that's no mistake like. He had a go agin' t'day and fortunately Billy interrupted the event and saved him from further embarrassment'

'You need to be careful there Em. I know you put him down and can handle all his crappy little comments like, but perhaps one day the worm will turn Pet ... and you could end up being in the wrong place at the wrong damn time'

Dave was serious; his newly formed expression confirming the fact.

'Me an' some o' the lads are on his case like' he continued: 'We'll catch him out one night, an circumstances might be such that we give him a right working over. Ye' know he's havin a go at young Kylie now ... an' she's just a kid Em. She's not as quick off the mark and as tough as you Pet ... in fact she's quite vulnerable. Ah'm telling ye', if he does anything to her like, he'll have all of us te' answer te"

'Aye, well Davey lad, youse'll all have te' bloody well queue up behind me like ... an ye could have te' wait a bit; I might just need te' take me time!'

Emily sipped at her second cup of tea. It was too hot and she considered adding some cold water. Mind reading Dave interrupted the thought.

'Would ' like me te' put a bit o' cold in that Pet ... cool it for ye' a bit like?'

'Aye, that would be nice Dave' Emily confirmed gratefully.

When he returned with the tea now drinkable, Emily had a question for him.

'A'h know we may have talked about this before, but remind me like, why have ye never gone for more schoolin like; gotten ye BTEC qualies and such?'

'Ah've told ye' before Em, me' folks have an on-line business; we've got a warehouse on that industrial estate behind the Port. They supply parts for industrial boilers. Me Dad was an engineer with the steelworks like, and when it closed he used the payoff money te' set up this on-line thing ... an it's doing very well'

'So, is that where you're going then ... will ye' leave here and go join em' like?'

'If A'h don't come te' London wi' you Em, I'll give it another year here and by then the family business should be able te' support me Mum an' Dad as well as me, full time like'

They both smiled at the quiet nudge about London, but Emily was not about to change her mind.

'So, ye' future's mapped out then. Ye' don't need any bits o' paper to get ye' a decent income'

'Oh no ... that's not the case Em. When A'h leave here I'm enrolling in the Open University an takin' a degree in Business Management. A'hve been through all the documentation like, an Ah've got it all sorted. Ah've learnt a lot about the tradin' business at Pertigrew's, not only how te' do things but more importantly how not te' do things. But don't say anything te' anybody else Em. I don't want te' have te' answer loads o' questions from al' the others like. Just keep it between us'

'Howay ye geet marra, ye secret's safe wi me man!'

The hand moved over once more and this time lingered a little longer.

'Ye' really are a dark horse Dave, Ah'm so bloody pleased for ye' an A'h know ye'll do well. Ye're a bright lad and that's no mistake like. Doin' Uni' will be great for ye' and ye'll meet some finer, better educated people like and not be suffocated by the moaning, bloody netty types and lazy bastards round here. That news has really made me' day ... and not only thanks fe' the biscuits, but thanks fe' that too!'

She leant forward across the table and kissed David lightly on the cheek, a cheek colouring immediately to a recognisable shade of crimson.

She smiled.

'Ye' see what ye' do te' me Em. Ah'm all of a bloody shiver now!'

'A'h read once somewhere Dave that a man wi'out ambition is like a beautiful worm ... it can creep like, but cannot fly'

'Oh, Ah've got ambition all right Em an one day it might make me enough money to come down to London like and buy the bloody store ye's working in ... and then ye'll have te marry me Pet'

They both burst out laughing.

The door to the floor opened unexpectedly. Billy appeared.

'When ye' two lovebirds ha' finished ye' tea, there's a few customers out here who would love ye' both to gi 'em the benefit of ye' many years o' experience in the hardware trade ... an' hopefully then they'll actually be persuaded te' damn well buy something!'

'Yes Boss! shouted David as the door closed shut.

'It'll soon be time to go Em' he said consulting the locker room clock again: '... and A'h suppose as its Friday, it'll be a night out wi' the girls for you'

'It will Dave ... it most certainly will!'

Chapter Eleven
4.00 pm

Emily knew well that shoplifting in the retail trade has always been a problem, but since the great financial crash of 2008 and the following dark days of so-called 'austerity' it had shown a significant increase. The illegal practice of basically walking out of the store with items that did not match a current receipt hit Pettigrew's to the tune of several thousand pounds a year and all staff were constantly being warned of the problem and to deal harshly with any suspects.

Vigilance was one thing, but mind reading was another. The way many of Pettigrew's customers were dressed when shopping would indicate anything from a homeless vagrant to a departmental manager at Marks and Spencer. People who walked through Pettigrew's doors were mainly in the building trade and as 'trade' customers they dressed to keep warm on a chilly, exposed building site rather than looking to be well placed in a local fashion contest. A lesser number could normally be identified as the much older and normally retired DIY enthusiast who would dress casually, sporting trade mark jeans with military standard ironed sharp creases.

There had never been a robbery as such at Pettigrew's. There had been many instances of shoplifting over the years, normally carried out by easily spottable, over confident teenagers or by middle aged professionals carrying shopping bags with aluminium foil linings. This was supposed to confuse the security tag readers designed to scan all goods as they left the store. However, out of three readers installed at the single exit, only one was known to work and that was generally unreliable. Lewis had been told about the situation on many occasions but for some unknown reason chose to ignore it. The only line of sensible defence for staff in the event of a show of force by shoplifters, or more adventurous thieves, was an emergency alarm button by the side of the till stations and a quick door closer. This activated the sliding door to rapid close mode and the alarm button logged up a robbery in progress at the nearby police station. Beneath each button was fixed a small green first aid box, all three of which were half empty, had been raided bare of sticking plaster over the years ... and never replaced.

So it was the two middle aged unshaven men who walked past Emily, standing guard on till number one, situated right next to the only entry and exit door to the premises for customers, looked as expected like workmen; safety boots, paint spattered overalls, mobile phone glued to the ear and a knitted beanie hat pulled down over the forehead. Staff all knew more than three quarters of Pettigrew's weekday customers were trade accounts; small contractors and self employed tradesmen. Therefore Emily gave them no second thought as the two passed hurriedly by, although noting she couldn't remember seeing them before. She looked absentmindedly out the door opening to register the fifteen year old rusting Ford Transit they had probably arrived in; nothing unusual there.

Billy, who patrolled the aisles in the hope he could assist some indecisive customer and guide them toward a sale, spotted the two engaged individuals who seemed to be moving through the store together, pausing here and there, but with no particular intent; no piece of paper in hand with a model number written on it, no sample of screw or other fixing requiring an accurate match. He thought nothing of it. If they still hadn't looked as if they were buying anything when he returned on his next patrol he would approach them and offer his services.

The two men spoke very little to one another and as soon a Billy disappeared out of sight, they changed aisles and moved to a display board holding a selection of bolt cutters. The slightly shorter one of the two quickly detached a pair and slipped them into the front bib pocket of his overalls. His partner moved down the aisle until he came to a section holding steel crow bars. These two were not simple shoplifters and the items taken were not what the devious pair were after. These were just the tools to do the job.

At the rear of the store, next to the door into the locker room, a display of expensive petrol driven concrete saws and disc cutters carried stock from some prime names such as Makita and Husqvarna. There were eight brand new models on display all secured to the steel stand with a series of chains. Next would come the distraction.

The two men, now 'tooled up', took the twenty or so paces that would bring them to a large free standing display board of hand tools at the very back of the shop; the farthest distance from the entrance. With little effort, they grabbed each end of the display and tipped it over. The noise, as the tools crashed to the tiled floor was horrendous and for the staff as confusing as it was unexpected. Billy stopped talking to a customer at the opposite end of the shop, trying to figure out what the hell had happened, whilst Emily had a feeling for the location and headed off in the direction of 'hand tools'.

When she arrived, her suspicions were confirmed. The complete display rack had somehow fallen over. Had it been stocked incorrectly? Had too much weight been stacked at the highest level making it top heavy? She shouted: 'Billy?'

No reply.

Emily shouted again: 'Billy?'

No reply.

It took only seconds for a quick witted Emily Macklam to figure out this mess in front of her was possibly a diversion for something more concerning.

Again she shouted: 'Billy ... fe' God's sake man ... answer me!'

Dave's voice answered: 'He's here Em ... by the front door. He's got a nasty gash on his nappa like ... an ... Jesus Christ, they're comin' back Em ... stay where ye' are!'

Emily moved as quickly as she could back to the entrance. Billy lay on the floor by till number two. He wasn't moving. David stood over him. She looked out to the car park. The rear doors to the old Transit were open and three new petrol saws lay in the back. The two thieves made no effort to disguise themselves; they were heading at a quickening pace back into the store, probably planning to steal the remaining saw stock.

'Shut the door Dave' she shouted, not taking her eyes off the leading robber.

Dave leapt for the button on the wall mounted control box. The glass doors began to slide closed. The lead robber had the crowbar in his hand. 'Press the alarm button David!' she instructed, her voice amazingly firm. Emily Macklam was now in control ... but would the doors, fitted with protective armoured glass, close and lock before the approaching thief reached them?

Just as the aluminium framed doors were about to close tight allowing the top and bottom locks to click into place, one end of the crow bar appeared between them, the face of the leading middle aged male robber up tight against the glass.

'Open the faar'kin door!' he shouted.

Emily moved closer to the door, now held open only by the levering action of the robber with his crowbar.

'Now don't ye' go usin' bad language like that Pet. We have a rule in this store, an' if ye's caught swearin' ... especially really bad words like ye' just used, then ye'll have to pay a fine ... me' handsome man!'

The threatening robber, ignoring Emily's warning of the certain consequences of swearing in Pettigrew's premises, repeated his demand, all the time struggling to lever open the motorised door. His partner appeared to be looking for something outside the store, something that could be used as a wedge or an item to add leverage to the short crowbar.

'Ye'll not be comin' in here Pet ... Ah've told ye' that, and ye's can shout all ye' like, but Ah've called the Polis an' they're only round the corner ...'

A familiar voice came from behind her.

'What's going on Em? Why's Billy on the floor and what are the doors shut for?'

It was the store manager, Peter Lewis who had obviously been disturbed by the internal alarm bell.

'We're bein' robbed Peter. Can ye' no see that? These two wankers think they're gettin' a second chance te' steal even more stock like, but A'hve told em' they're not comin' back in here!'

With continuing persistence, the robber working the crow bar had managed to get his foot in the gap between the two doors, a gap that was undoubtedly getting bigger.

'Leave it!' shouted a pale faced Lewis: 'I'll only tell you once. Leave it Em; let them take what they want. Get upstairs with me to the office ... NOW!'

'A'hm not leaving Billy here on the bloody floor wi' these two lunatics outside, so do what ye' want Peter, but these two bastards are not comin' in here ... an' that's a fact Pet!'

At that, the manager, with a face like thunder, turned on his heel and at a fast walk headed for the stairs leading back up to the main office, slamming the door behind him.

Emily looked toward Billy being attended to by David. He was moving. That must have been a good sign. He was trying to stand but David gently pushed him back to the floor.

The robber at the door continued to scream threats at Emily, the tone rising higher and higher in an accent labelling his upbringing to be substantially further south than Hartlepool.

'Are ye' bloody doylem's southerners?' she shouted: 'What's up like ... have ye' run so short o' bloody disc cutters down there that ye' have te' come up here an' nick ours?'

'Listen you mad bitch ... open this faa'rkin door because one way or another, we're coming in ... and when we do I'm going to see to you lady ... you'll wish you'd never been born!'

At that point, the second 'doylem' appeared waving a ten foot deck board around. He shouted to his friend with his foot in the door. It could only have been a second or two of distraction ... but it was enough. Emily leapt forward, hand outstretched, reaching for the curved end of the crowbar, grabbed it and then pulled on it with all her might; pulling so hard she fell backward with the momentum. David watched it all happen and rushed over to help her up ... crowbar in hand.

The robber had perhaps somehow been shocked into silence. How had that happened? He had lost his weapon and perhaps with it some of his courage as from over his shoulder his partner rammed the end of the deck board in the remaining door gap, forced open by a booted foot.

Emily, now standing and with one heavy steel crowbar in hand, moved quickly to get nearer to the door.

She spat the words at the now silent, red faced and momentarily trapped raider.

'I hope ye've got steel toecaps in them boots ye' geet' wazzock, 'cause if not ... this is goin' te' hurt like!'

Emily raised the crowbar above her head and brought it down, with all her strength, on the foot of the now speechless robber. The contact appeared to be good; much better that Emily expected and the result, judging by the scream of pain bursting through the gap in the door confirmed to Emily the exercise had been worthwhile.

That was the point at which the whole event began to deteriorate, appearing as a yet to be released scene from 'The Plank'. The injured thief, as some sort of reaction to Emily's attack attempted to jump backwards with the back of his head making contact with the nose of his partner holding the timber deck board. He dropped the length of timber in a rush to bring a hand up to his bleeding nose with the end springing up and hitting the robber trapped in the door squarely on the side of his head.

David checked quickly back in Billy's direction, He was half standing but managing without help. It looked as if he would be OK, so David was now eager to become involved.

'Gi' me that bloody crowbar Em!' he shouted.

She handed it over with a warning.

'Now don't ye' go doin' anything silly Dave. Ye' know these southerners are a bit soft like ... an' this one here owes money for the damn swear box!'

'Well, he's goin' te' owe a wee bit more in a minute Em. Just stand back a bit Pet ... A'h want to get a good swing at it like!'

'OK, but A'h want another go ... after this one ...!'

With that, a fit, seventeen stone David swung the crowbar down with eye watering force and like Emily, made perfect contact with the trapped boot poking through the gap in the door. A distinct crack could be heard indicating a possible broken bone or two as the screams of pain became nearly loud enough to wipe out the continuing urgent sound of the droning alarm bell.

With Billy now recovered and on his feet he joined David and Emily to assess the situation. Police sirens could be heard in the distance.

The bold raider with his foot in the door was now on the floor with the leg attached to his trapped foot appearing to be settled at an unusual angle. His partner to the rear had been left desperately attempting to stem the flow of blood from what appeared to be a badly injured nose.

Half a minute later a police car swept into the car park and for Emily and David, the fun was now over.

But was it fun? Now the truth, the reality of what had just happened was beginning to sink in and the shaking started. David and Emily hugged one another and a thankfully 'compos mentis' Billy patted them both on the back.

Two more police cars appeared in short succession. One of the officers came over to Billy.

'Are you the manager?' he asked.

'Haddaway, man ... that particular southern twat ye' looking for can probably be found upstairs, barricaded in his office wi' his female staff guarding his bloody door!'

'Are there any more about?'

'No' replied Emily: 'A'h saw em' when they came in, an' there were only two o' em'. Them's southerners A'h think; come up here to rob us easy targets like ... as if we don't have enough damned robbing bastards of our own! That vehicle there, wi' the back doors open is theirs an A'h think we'll want our saws back afore ye' take it away'

'We'll need a statement' the young officer confirmed.

'Aye, well ye' can have what the hell ye' want lad when my mate Billy has his wounds seen to Pet. So pop off an' find us someone dressed in green ... an' then A'hm all yours!'

The young policeman smiled along with a much improved Billy and a greatly relieved David.

Chapter Twelve
5.00 pm

With a lot of clearing up to do in the store, Emily wondered if she would get away on time at five thirty. The 'southern twat' as Billy noted to other members of staff, was holding court in the office giving a full and detailed statement to a police sergeant who seemed unimpressed with its mainly fictional content. A police woman who arrived in the second car however, had taken a very obvious interest in Emily. She had given her statement. Both thieves had been captured, the van recovered and the stolen contents taken away for evidence.

Joan, the thirty something year old police woman with a Yorkshire accent, felt it her duty to take some time with Emily's statement in order to ensure her description of the way she attacked the raider with the trapped foot fell into the category of self defence rather than grievous bodily harm.

'He can sue you Emily, you know that don't you? If your actions have caused him serious harm then a smart mouthed young solicitor might just advise him to sue you ... as an individual and probably the store as an entity'

'Howay Joan! Ye canna' tell me this bloody robber can come inta' the store like, steal from us, cause soddin' mahem ... an' then sue me for tryin' to stop him? A'h mean ... that's bloody ridiculous like ... bloody ridiculous Pet!'

'Well, one thing we must do is emphasize the threat from these two crims and the way you actually felt at the time; being threatened, frightened of what might happen to you, the language he used to you ... and all that kind of thing'

'A'h canna believe what you're telling me Joan. A'h simply canna' believe it like!'

'I have to say it's a good job your friend David also took a swing at him because if there is significant physical damage to this assholes foot, then it will be difficult, in court, to prove which blows, delivered by which individual caused the damage'

Emily fell silent. She looked over toward till station two where David was also giving a statement and no doubt receiving the same advice from Constable Joan's working partner. David raised his eyebrows and shrugged. He was obviously getting the same disagreeable message.

'Can't we gi' a statement together Pet? We were both there ... an' then we could make sure the statements matched like'

'That's the last thing we want Emily. Each of your statements must tell the same story, but not in the same words. Don't worry, we will guide you through it but it is important this very first statement fits the bill as this will be the one that influences any later decision to prosecute. Do you understand?' Joan explained.

'Aye, A'h do that Pet. Let's bloody well get on wi' it'

'You're a tough young lady' commented the policewoman with a smile in her voice: 'You know we have your brother down at the nick don't you? Its time he understood he's getting older and it won't be a 'kids' warning or young offenders place any more, it'll be the real thing ... and I can tell you Emily, he won't like it'

'Look Joan ... if A'h hear one more bloody word about our Thomas, A'h tell ye, Ah'll just get on a bloody train and get me'sel outa' here. Ah'm fed up wi' it all. Ah'm not his keeper! A'h keep on tellin' people that! You's lot need te' get me Ma off her arse an out the house an down the damn station and sortin' im out like. A'h canna do it ... an A'h won't go surety for im. Ah'm only nineteen for god's sake. Ah've got a life o' me own to lead. Do ye understand Joan ... Ah've a life o' me own to live!'

'OK ... OK Emily ... I know where you're coming from. I just have to tell you that's all and it wouldn't be a problem but we have no safe place to put him and we certainly can't send him home ... unless you can go guarantor for him ...'

Joan paused, waiting to see if Emily would finally cave in. She was about to be disappointed.

'Just get on wi' the bloody statement Joan ... and do me a favour like an' don't mention that bloody tosser's name to me again!'

In the office, with his stage performance for the benefit of the local constabulary now finished, Peter Lewis had Billy in front of him, quizzing him about the real turn of events.

'A'h don't care what ye' say ... or anyone else fe' that matter, our Emily deserves a bloody medal fe' what she did today!'

There will be no damn medals handed out here Billy ... only reprimands!' offered an angry Lewis.

'Reprimands ...?' echoed a disbelieving Billy Saunders.

'Absolutely!' shouted the manager: 'I told her to come upstairs with me ... and she disobeyed me ... so that's the first thing. Secondly, the police say there may be legal action taken against the company if the guy who had his foot damaged by the reckless behaviour of Emily Macklam has suffered any major injury!'

'Are ye' off ye' bloody head man? If it wern't for Em you'd ha' lost a lot of bloody stock and probably had more people hurt or me finished off fe' good like! De' ye not understand that ye' bloody idiot!'

Billy was angry. All the office staff turned in the direction of the goldfish bowl. None of them had seen Billy angry before.

'Well, Ah'm tellin' ye' Mister bloody high an' mighty Lewis, if ye send in a bad report about Em or make any move to reprimand her ... Ah'll be round ye' house like tellin' ye' missus what a leching little bastard ye are an' Ah'll have the evidence standing right by me side when A'h do it an' all. So you think on lad ... you think on afore ye do anything ye' might regret!' With that, Billy left the office, storming past the cringing accountant.

'And what the hell are you lot all gawping at?' Lewis shouted at a sea of faces all turned in his direction. Perhaps they knew something could possibly be about to happen now. It had been building for some time. The 'southern twat' had dropped his guard and now the office staff wondered what the consequences would be. The faithful, led by an adoring Harriet Pearson, thought this one simple incident of disrespect could blossom into something rather bigger, perhaps leading to the dismissal of the unattractive and disinterested Billy Saunders. The poker faced Jane Witham, however, had another theory and this involved the leaking of an anonymous, much embellished and biased account of events to head office and the desk of Jonothan Pettigrew himself. The 'southern twat' as everyone now indirectly referred to him, could be gone within a week! Maybe even a bonus could be extracted from the whole situation by making sure the annoying, aloof and 'mutton dressed as lamb' Harriet Pearson went with him!

Emily caught the ten to six bus home. She knew one or two of the other passengers. One in particular was eager to sit beside her; a twenty year old with two kids, not a husband in sight and a semi adequate living made by social security payments, backed up with a little bit of regular shop lifting. She stole mainly to order, often using her two young children and various accessories, such as push chairs and large hand bags, as cover.

Taylor Donohue spent her days either trying to sell something to someone or soliciting a requirement from someone with a plan to eventually make them a regular customer ... at 'mates rates'. Taylor had no children with her that day but she did have the trade mark giant shopping bag, looking worryingly cumbersome, parked on the seat opposite. Emily knew that no matter how any conversation began with Taylor, it would eventually end up with a hard sell for some ladies toiletries or a pair of top line 'something or other can't live without item', relatively compact, easily concealable ... and only just arrived on the shelves at Curry's PC World.

'A'h were walkin' past your place earlier and A'h saw the polis there ... in some force like! When A'h saw em, A'h thought to me'sel, them polis are there in force like, Em. They wern't comin for you were they Pet cause when A'h saw em, A'h thought to me'sel, perhaps they've come for Em like, wanting to know where her skanky brother is ... or something ... like!'

'No Taylor Pet. It were a couple o' gangsters from down south who fancied their chances. The rozzers told me they lived in London like, but travelled up north, did a few robberies then went back south again. The local Polis been lookin' for em' for some time'

'Well, that's good then' confirmed an unconvinced Taylor Donohue: 'Perhaps they'll keep the bastards off the back's o' poor people like me who's only try'in to bring up me kids sensible an earn a decent livin' like!'

Emily sighed. She was not in the mood for Taylor today. In effect she was still recovering from the experience of a couple of hours earlier. It had taken several minutes to finally stop shaking and a strong cup of tea to restore a sense of perspective to the complete series of events.

Peter Lewis had only spoken to her once as the Police carted away the two store raiders. He had placed a light tap on her shoulder, arm extended, careful not to get too close, muttering 'Well done Em' as he passed by playing the role of 'manager in full charge' now the danger was over. The police had seen it all and so had the two paramedics who came to attend to Billy's knock on the head.

Taylor had not stopped talking.

'So, A'h saw these lovely new heated tongs Ah'd seen on telly sitting there in Curry's Em, an A'h thought to me'sel like, well there's them lovely new heated tongs A'h just seen on telly ... sittin there, on the shelf, in Curry's!'

'A'h don't need any tongs Taylor' Emily advised knowing that a full sales pitch could be underway at any moment.

'Well, A'h don't know if ye saw them tongs on

telly the other night Em, but A'h got some, an' they come in that nice pinky sort o' colour like ... here, have a quick peek Pet ...'

With that, Taylor pulled a box out of the large parked shopping bag.

'These a' little gem's Em. Brand new; they's are over fifty quid in Curry's like an I can do one for ye for less than half that ... an there's a guarantee like ... ye' just have te' fill in a form ... an' send it off!'

'Does that mean you're actually writing to the company who make's em' to confirm you're the one who stole em?'

'A'h don't get ye' like. How, by fillin' a form would that tell anybody they've been stole like?'

'Cause Taylor, the shop will register the serial number of the goods when they sell em'. When they take stock, any goods wi' a serial number that's not gone through the till and not left on the shelf ... has been stolen Pet!'

Taylor gave the matter some serious thought. She was not dumb by any standards, but it sometimes took a while for the penny to drop.

'Well now, I've learnt somat' t'day like' she said eventually, but still not totally convinced: 'Ye mean that tellin' people to register for a warranty like is probably the wrong thing te' do then ... is that what ye' tryin' te' tell me Em?'

'That's what A'h mean Taylor. Just stick with the discounted price; don't mention the bloody warranty and make sure your fingerprints are not on the damn box!'

'Taylor smiled.

'You an' me ought to go in'te business Pet ...'

'No thanks' Em interrupted: 'It's enough A'h have te' do keepin' me brother on the straight and narrow like, wi'out takin' you on as well'

'Well, as a sign of me good faith like an' just 'cause ye've helped me out Em, A'h can do these top line heated curling tongs, fresh off the shelf at Curry's for a special low price ... and just for ye' like ... for ten pound. Now that's a crackin offer Pet. Ye' won't get that on bloody Amazon ... I can tell ye' ...'

'Much as A'h love ye Taylor, an' A'h suppose in some ways admire ye like for fightin to put clothes on ye kids back, Ah'm not buyin' anything from ye' today ... whether it be nicked or kosher. De ye understand Pet ... not today!'

'Oh well, ye' get nothing if ye' don't try Em'

'That's true Taylor ... that's oh so bloody true!' confirmed a thoughtful Emily.

Chapter Thirteen
6.00 pm

The house was a mess although not quite as bad as expected. Emily checked the time; ten past six. She would need to tidy up and get ready. She had a few pounds in her pocket, a new dress from her favourite town centre charity shop with a cut that fitted her like a glove and showed off an exceptionally fine pair of legs. She had not worn it before but as a 'leg advert' it couldn't possibly be beaten. The top half however was another matter with buttons controlling the amount of flesh on view.

'Get up Ma ... get y'sel up for God's sake!' Emily shouted as she discovered her mother sprawled across the kitchen floor. The house, although in some distress, had hopefully maintained its secret and Emily moved quickly upstairs to check the day's hiding place. She had used the bath panel before, but not for some months and as soon as she entered the bathroom she could see it had not been moved. Pulling back the bottom corner, lifting the fibreglass cover gently, a small cling-film wrapped bundle, containing one ten pound and three twenty pound notes, fell to the floor.

'Great' Emily whispered, as she pushed the bundle back and replaced the panel. There would hopefully be some food in the house tomorrow.

Back in the kitchen, Emily watched, wanting to help but daring not to do so, as her mother levered herself up on a kitchen chair and then catching hold of the table, guided herself into a relatively upright sitting position. The track suit top had a fresh stain down the front; no doubt another wasted attempt at making coffee.

She'd had a lot of drink ... Emily was certain of the fact, but it hadn't been purchased with the housekeeping, so that in itself was a blessing.

'What ye' doin' on the damned floor Ma?' Emily asked.

'A'h just slipped like, probably on the mess ye' left on the floor this morning Pet!'

'A'h left nee' mess Ma ... it's more than likely ye' scummy mates ye've had round ha' left a mess cause I see someone's bin' feedin' ye' drink today like'

Eva Macklam reached across the kitchen table for a pack of cigarettes and a lighter. She took one out of the packet and lit up.

Emily hated the cinder smell of cigarette smoke. She had never taken up the filthy habit and neither had any of her friends. Thomas however was another story. It was an expensive addiction and he would need to steal, shoplift and sometimes even bully other boys into parting with money in order to maintain an uninterrupted supply. To him it was just being part of the 'in crowd' and showing off with his immature mates. However, he had not seen Jack Macklam in the last horrific stages of his life literally pouring his lungs, his black tar soaked and bleeding lungs down the damn sink; had not smelt the evidence; had not had to bloody well clean it up. If he had, he would never have set fire to a 'tab' in his life.

'A'h had nee' snout Em ... an Davie from down' the road brought me some like ...'

'Aye Ma, an' a bottle of White Lightnin' too by the bloody look of it!'

The empty two litre bottle, the evidence of the conclusion rested where it had fallen, by the side of the fridge.

'Well, A'h can't stand here gassin' wi' you al' day like, Ah'm out the neet an A'h have te' get ready'

'Well, ye' brother won't have that pleasure t'day like ... will he Pet?'

Signs of bitterness crept into Eva's face as she carefully delivered the words, drawing on her cigarette and blowing smoke defiantly in Emily's direction. When coming into direct conflict with her mother, Emily knew to count to ten before engaging in any form of acid verbal exchange. Such altercations normally ended up in tears and no matter what she realistically thought of her mother's situation, Eva Macklam was her mother and no daughter wanted to see her mother cry.

'Ah'm not getting in'te it wi' ye' Ma. If ye' want te' change the situation, then best ye' change in'te another tracksuit top like, one wi'out bloody tea al' over it and get ye'sel down the cop shop. But let me tell ye Ma, they'll not release him to ye' ... cause ye's a drunk Ma ... and that's why he's like he is. Until ye' damn well change ... then there's nee' bloody hope in hell for him like! De' ye' not see that Ma ... de' ye' not bloody well see that!'

Eva stared at the kitchen table, puffing mechanically at the cigarette. She looked up searching for eye contact with her daughter; no sign of a building tear. With a connection made, for a brief second, Emily felt her mother was about to shout out: 'I'll do it ... I'll give up the demon drink ... I'll do it Em ...!' Certainly something was going on behind the eyes; eyes providing a brief window into a confused mind; eyes that had lost any sign of motherly friendliness. Then, with only a second or two's pause, the connection filtered away to be replaced by a regular blank, brooding look.

'Ye don't tret' me right Em. I'm ye' mother ... an ye' don't tret' me right ... that's all A'h can say like. Ah've spoke to the polis an' they've told me ye' won't go down an' see him. That's terrible Em ... ye' own bother like'

'A'h keep telling ye, he's not me damn brother is he Ma ... 'caus ye' couldn't wait till me Da died before ye' had to go out shaggin' like. That's the problem wi' that boy; ye' won't damn well admit me Da is not his Da ... and he needs to face up to it Ma. Ye' need to sort it out like ... and A'h mean right now or else they'll be no savin' im'. De ye' understand ... no savin' im!'

It was too much. She knew it. As soon as the subject of Thomas' full parenthood came up, her mother retreated into a shell that would only be broken open by a litre bottle of Whiskey or several substantial intakes of cheap gut destroying cider.

'A'h can't stand no more o' this Ma. I've got a bloody life te' lead of me own; A'h do my best in this house Ma ... me level best ... and that son of YOURS Ma ... not that brother of MINE will have to take his bloody chances like the rest o' us!'

The first tear fell making an audible sound as it hit the kitchen table breaking a short vacuum of silence. Many would now follow, probably in quick succession and then would come the muttering, the self pity and eventually the manic shouting and screaming at her nineteen year old daughter to get her some more damned drink.

Emily turned away. Sod tiding up the house. Now was the time to lock herself in her room, her refuge, her place of safety and get ready for a night out with an ambition to make it better than the best one so far.

Grabbing her phone, hands trembling slightly, but emotions fully under control, she searched for 'Nell' and when the name came up she stabbed at it with her finger.

Nellie Curtis was considered by Emily to be her best friend. She was a tad older in physical years but they were well matched in maturity and an agreed need to 'break the mould' whenever the opportunity became available. She had a car and with the car came independence. She had a job, and with that job came financial security. She had a slightly dilapidated but perfectly functional rented flat in the next village to Emily's and all this achieved at the tender age of twenty four. Tonight, Emily and Nell would be out 'on the town' and when the full gang of mates, numbering possibly eight in all, were gathered together with a few drinks inside them, they would become a formidable group and one most young men without a rhino hard skin would be advised to avoid.

'So, ye' pickin' us up Nell?' Emily queried.

'No problem Pet. About seven if that's OK'

'That'll be fine Nell. A'll be ready. A'h need te' get outa' this damn place tonight. Me Ma's throwin' one like an' A'h canna take ne' more of this family shit right now'

'Don't ye worry bonnie lass, A'h think there'll be a full house tonight like. Everybody's meetin' up at the Jolly Sailor an' then after a quick tour of a few pub's in toon we're planning to hit the Marina ... an' gi' it a bit o' wellie wi' some smooth dance moves like. Are ye' up for it Pet?'

'Ye can count me in on that Nell'

'Right then, ye' just squezze inta' ya' sexiest underwear an' make sure ye' have a spare pair o' knickers an' a rubber raincoat in ye' handbag. If ye' get lucky tonight Pet you'll probably need both!'

Emily smiled.

'A'll see ye' at seven Nell ... can't wait'

Throwing the phone on the bed Emily Macklam sat at the small set of freestanding drawers serving as a dressing table, topped with an inadequately sized and cracked mirror precariously balanced, leaning against the wall. She stared at her reflection for a long moment, considering perhaps what her life had been about so far and where on earth it would possibly be going in the future.

The face in the mirror often talked back to her. Sometimes it said: 'keep calm' and on other occasions it said: 'go for it' but never did it say: 'give up!' The past couple of years of work and study, housework and cleaning up sick, budget management and failed mentoring of a reckless child had taken its toll. Yes, there had been times when she just wanted to damn well give up ... throw it all to the bloody wind, But as her life progressed, as each month inched by, she grew stronger and more determined. She would be leaving this damn place ... and when she did, she would never be coming back.

Emily had no real problem with Hartlepool or the people in it. In fact, like many others, she felt it was a welcoming place with great shopping, great social life and a surrounding countryside the envy of many other towns in a similar position. With the bitter taste of closing coal mines and rusting steelworks lingering in many older mouths there was now a new town with new ambitions inhabited by young people with a determination to change old identities and shake off the bitterness of the past. If anything, this was just the place for an ambitious nineteen year old to create a new persona, seek plentiful educational opportunities and take home a regularly fattening pay packet.

However, for Emily, Hartlepool was not the real problem. The challenge of managing a home, a drunken mother and delinquent brother had been too much; she was exhausted and completely brain numbed. She knew for sure that if she lived within fifty miles of her mother and brother, they would seek her out and hang their 'dirty washing' at her door. She would never be rid of them. The phone calls would never end, visits from police would never end and heated conversations with eighteen year old social services busybodies would pursue her for the rest of her life.

No, she had to go and make sure it was a long, long way from Hartlepool. She had money in the bank, enough to set her up in London. She had no illusions about how hard it would be but she had made a few visits to the capital over the past year often with her friend Nell and was confident she could handle the underground system and had accepted that most styles of frothy coffee would set her back three and a half quid and a pint of semi decent beer close to five.

Emily had also learnt that signing up with London agencies or writing letters to companies when looking for a job was not the way to go. As the result of a one night stand with a rather attractive recruitment executive name Bob, at least that's what he called himself, she knew for sure the only way to get on the employment ladder was to turn up at the front door of a business and simply knock on it. Bob put it quite plainly. Unfortunately, as part of his advice, he saw it as still very much a man's world, especially down in the big 'smoke', therefore there was a game to be played and if played intelligently, then the world could be Emily's oyster.

'Looking like you do darlin' guarantees the first door you knock on will undoubtedly open ... and then it's just down to charm and long hours! When you do eventually decide to come to London and ready to work, look me up ... maybe there are a couple of doors I could open for you myself ... and no favours required!'

There was some concern of course. Moving south, lock, stock and barrel required not only guts but a conviction that she could make a success of her life, a success that would bring her some form of financial stability. The thatched cottage, white painted picket fence, handsome hard working husband and two point three children did not interest her. A wealthy husband was not on her list of needs and if she wanted one, there were plenty of wealthy 'pillocks' up here in the north. Emily Macklam was just a restless soul; that's what she told herself and that's what she believed. Staying where she was could never be considered an option and her solid conviction of the fact had worried her best friend Nell. At one point, Nell had perhaps considered moving south with her, but for all of her tough and unforgiving exterior, she was not made of the same stuff as Emily.

She finished her flawless makeup and patted down the tight fitting dress for the twentieth time, turning round and round in front of her mirror. 'It would do' she assured herself ... 'It would do!'

With all the essentials in her handbag and a comfortable pair of heels to finish off her outfit, Emily Macklam would shortly be one of 'the girls' and any men who fancied their chances tonight, had better be prepared for a rough ride!

The muffled sound of her mother screaming and shouting downstairs could be heard over the smashing of the odd plate or maybe a mug or china teacup. Another five minutes and she would be quieter. A further five and she would be back to her normal morose but calmer state where literally nothing happening around her would register unless it was the smell of an open bottle of whiskey. Within an hour, the kitchen would smell of freely released farts and pee. Would Emily make any sort of effort to clean up the house before she left on her 'girls night out'? 'No' would be the answer ... a very firm 'No' indeed. It was Friday. It was HER night and whatever went on in this house between now and eight o'clock tomorrow morning was none of her concern. This was the way Emily Macklam controlled her sanity ... and it was the only medicine she needed!

She turned her attention back to the mirror and the makeup. When she left that house, that night, she wouldn't necessarily look a million dollars ... but she sure as hell would not be too far away. Whoever managed to sweet talk this northern girl into bed tonight ... would be a very lucky man indeed!

Chapter Fourteen
7.00 pm

The journey to town would take half an hour; a useful time to catch up with the latest gossip. Emily had experienced an interesting day what with the rejected advances from her manager, the foiled robbery attempt at the store and her brother's continuing criminal activity.

'A'h told that bloody wazzock Peter Lewis te' get howay man an gi' his wife a bit o' attention like rather than chasin' after young innocent girls like me!'

'Aye ... an' what de' he say to that like?'

'Well Nell ... he wanted te' talk about somethin' hard he said'

'Hard? Surely the only thing hard about 'im is the shit in his toenails Pet'

'Well he was pretty sure mind; he definitely said he had something hard te' show me ... an' if Billy hadn't interrupted us, A'h feel quite sure he would have got it out like ... te show me!'

'Before he could show it t'e ye' Pet, he would have to bloody well find it and even wi' trousers as tight as his like A'h think ye would need a satellite navigation ... an a last known address!'

Both girls laughed out loud. Nell had been kept pretty well up to date with Lewis' inept and fumbling attempts to get inside Emily's knickers and when told about the latest failure, Emily knew her best friend would have had a suitable and amusing opinion to put forward.

'But what about your Thomas Em? What's

happenin' wi' him like?'

'A'h really don't know Pet. That Polis woman Shelly cornered me today. She keeps tryin' te' get me te' do something wi' Thomas like but what the hell can A'h do that won't tie him to my bloody apron strings for the rest of his life like? Me Ma's got te' sort hersel' out and then sort im' out. A'h simply can't get involved wi' the little shit. He does'na know who is Da is and that would be a damn starting point for im' like. She's in total bloody denial, the house is like a damn pigsty and we have a boy who thinks he's a man on his way to spendin' the best part of his life in prison. It's a shit-storm Nell ... a complete bloody shit-storm'

Emily's best friend fell silent, absorbing the obvious emotion and anxiety being transmitted by someone who cared, but dare not care, for a family destined to disintegrate no matter what efforts were to be made by people like PC Shelly. If Emily's mother continued drinking at her present rate, Nell knew the future for her looked gloomy indeed. If her delinquent brother, with a massive chip on his shoulder, continued stealing cars and joyriding round Cleveland, then one day his luck would probably run out and he would find himself standing in the dock on a manslaughter charge or even worse ... delivered home in a wooden box.

'Ye just gotta' keep ye' head up Pet' offered Nell: 'Ye Ma won't listen to ye' Em 'cause you're her daughter an' mother's never listen to their daughters ... that's a damn fact. Unless she tells Thomas about his history, who is Da is an' all, then nothin's goin' te' be right in ya' hyam, he's going te' al'ways be up a height like'

Emily found her determined face and turned it toward Nell.

'A'h just divvin care nay'more Nell. A'hm ganna' gi' that London a try like when A'h get me certificates. Then, they can both de' as they like. A'h just wan'te get on wi' me life Nell. A'h want te' leave al' this shit behind me ... and get on wi' me damn life!'

'Ye have te' do what ye' have te' do Pet. As ye' say, it's ye' own damn life an' ye' must lead it as ye' see it ... A'hm right behind ye' there Pet'

'Thanks Nell ... just te' have at least one person te' rely on means a lot'

'Nee' bother Pet ... now tell me about the robber!'

Both girls smiled with Emily taking a breath, holding back full blown laughter.

'Well, these two wazzock's came in'te the store like and wandered around for a bit. They looked the part like. A'h mean just like real workmen, the kind we have comin' through the doors everyday Nell. The plan was right good an' te' divert attention they knocked over a big hand tool display. It made a hell of a noise an' we al' came rushin' to see what's happenin' like. They had nicked some bolt cutters an' whilst we was wondering what had happened, they cut away some petrol disc cutters ... worth quite a bit o' money.

Te' cut a long story short, they were'nt satisfied wi' just one go at it, they were comin' back for more when I spotted em' and told Dave te' close the doors like. Well, the first idiot got his foot caught in the door and he started swearin' at me Nell ... right got me back up Pet ... an' then he kept pushin' this bloody crowbar though the door, so I grabbed it like an' then smashed his foot wi' it!. Then he definitely was swearin' ... but by that time I could hear he was a southerner ... an' one wi'out a very large swearin' vocabulary ... not like a much more reliable northern robber like!'

Nell could no longer hold back laughter.

'So, this useless bastard is stuck wi his foot in the door ... and you're bashin' at it wi' a crowbar ... it's like som'at from a Keystone Cops movie Pet'

'Well, it gets worse. He's shoutin' at me te' open the effin' door and Ah'm tellin im' Ah'm not like ... an then Dave grabs the crowbar and brings it down on the trapped foot wi an almighty crack. Dave said the robbin' bastard's scream will haunt 'im for the rest o' his life!'

'Stop Em ... I'm gonna be in tears in a mo ...'

'No, there's more Nell. In-between me hitting im' and Dave hittin' him, his dumb arsed mate turned up wi' a plank of wood to prise open the door a bit more like, and he wa' stood right behind his trapped mate. When A'h hit the one wi' the trapped foot wi' the crowbar, his head jumped back like and smashed his partner in the nose ... an must a' broke it like 'cause there was blood and shit everywhere. As he dropped the plank to grab his bleeding nose, it hit the trapped one on the head and then they were both on the floor ... just as the bloody Polis turned up ...'

Nell was now in fits of laughter, picturing the scene as described by an excited and over-animated Emily.

'Now, would ye' get ye' wee head round this Nell? Some bloody Polis woman tell'ed me that A'h had te' be careful what A'h said in case the robbin' shit's wanted to sue me for GBH like. A'h could'na believe it Nell ... A'h really could'na believe it!'

'Oh dear, oh dear' said Nell, wiping tears from her face.

'An where was ye' great and bold manager when al' this was happenin' Em? Was he getting involved like?'

'Was he buggery Pet. He sat barricaded in his damn office with his 'girls' for protection and as soon as the boys in blue arrived, you would have thought he had personally taken them robbers on single handed like. He's just a pillock Nell ... a bloody great pillock'

'So, changin' the subject for a we moment Nell, we're goin' te' the Jolly Sailor first ... is that right?'

'Aye, it is Em. The rest o' the girls will be there by eight. We'll have a couple o' pints there like an then gi' a taxi te' the Marina. I'll leave me car in the car park an' pick it up te'morra'

'That sounds like a plan babe ... that sounds like a plan!'

'What happens if ye get a pull like?' Emily asked.

'Well, A'hve got me taxi fare separate in me purse Pet and knowing ye' as A'h do, A'h suppose ye'll have the same'

'Damn right Nell ... standard accessories; a spare pair o' knickers, a couple o' rubber raincoats an' taxi fare home. All present and correct Madam!'

'Good, well if we get separated later, don't forget t' ring me te'morra like an let me know you're al'right'

'I will Nell ... and you make sure ye look after ye'sel too!'

The Jolly Sailor was a Pub more or less in the middle of town. It was a regular meeting place for the young and the not so young. Friday and Saturday nights delivered live music to the faithful and by eight o'clock, getting a table was not an option. Nell knew the landlord well, a thirty something divorcee who had a bit of a 'thing' for the tall brunette with a friendly smile and a sharp tongue. Tony would make sure there was a table for Nell and 'the girls' and as Emily and Nell walked in he indicated with a wave of the arm a large circular table in the window. It had a 'reserved' sign on it.

Nell blew the landlord a kiss and he coloured slightly, attempting to avoid her lingering gaze.

'Ye not goin' te' give him one tonight are ye' Nell?'

'Howay man! ... it's not his night ... unless he get's particularly lucky like. Midweek maybe, if Ah'm feelin a bit horny ... but not normally at the weekend Pet. Friday night is for lookin' round Em, a bit like shoppin, havin a good look ... and maybe even feel the goods a bit, te' get the measure of em' like ... but not necessarily buying the bloody sales pitch ... ye' know the score Em!'

'Aye, A'h know the score Nell' confirmed Emily checking her watch; ten to eight ... time to get a drink in.

As they sat down, four more of the 'team' arrived with news the last two were on their way ... and to get a pint in.

With eight pints of Cameron's Ruby Red on the table the last two sat down and the night's entertainment was about to begin.

Chapter Fifteen
8.00 pm

With an hour to go before the first band of the night planned to start hammering away at taut guitar strings, the Pub began to fill up. The 'girls' would all be sitting down, having a 'chat' together and the 'boys' would generally be up for a bit of exposure, leaning against the bar with their wares on full view in the hope that any of the good looking young ladies present would be giving out an invitational 'eye'. This would not include the partner they may be attending with of course. It was a bit of a game, and most knew how to play it.

The various levels of macho-ness, as demonstrated by the antics played out by youths glued to the bar with wandering eye and hormone driven poses, could be scored from one to ten. The younger amongst them were probably all under drinking age. Some looked as if they had made quite admirable attempts to cover acne infested faces; the popular formulae being liberal applications of the best makeup available from the popular Boots quick cover, unscented range. The trend of slashing the knees out of a pair of jeans with a razor blade had been around for some time and out of touch fashion conscious young men had now taken the whole thing too far. This extremely draughty version would leave the top half of a leg more or less completely disconnected from the bottom and much care would be needed when manipulating them in confined spaces or outside with a fair wind blowing.

However, this was the North East on a Friday night and the picture would be the same in just about any pub or public place where young men and young ladies would normally gather. Some of course would be standing at the bar with their current 'beloved' but this would not normally deter the proud male from casting his net in case a better looking 'fish' could be caught with a sideways glance, an inviting wink or even a loose hand massaging a gyrating crutch. With a persisting myth the North East boasted the highest teen pregnancy rates in the country anyone visiting the bar at the Jolly Sailor that night, and taking one look at some of the brainless youths propping it up, would immediately know why.

The most impressionable of Emily's particular group was Tonia Biggs, a cute eighteen year old who dressed well, could not hold her drink and definitely appeared unable to resist a well delivered, flattering line. Janice Potter, married and now safely separated from a cheating, drunken husband, also looked for Friday night to satisfy a regular physical urge. However, that did not mean she wasn't choosy because she definitely was. She had a good line of chat herself and looked for men not from the local area. She had had enough of that. Her targets were more mature guys, such as contractors working in the locality for a few weeks at a time, or at the other end of the scale, foreign students looking to break their particular duck. The other girls nurtured no particular strengths or weaknesses. They were just looking for a good night out; lots of girlie banter and words of encouragement for as many virgin youths as they could possible capture. Friday nights were not necessarily a ritual for Emily and Nell's team, but it was getting to be that way. A straw poll of just about every punter in the bar at the Jolly Sailor that night would have revealed individuals with problems; issues around social care, even more issues around the blasphemously named Universal Credit and an urge to change their circumstances. However, this was the North East, a place where everyone was constantly being told by government agencies, TV reporters and joke spewing comedians alike that this was the poorest and most socially disadvantaged place in Britain. Emily Macklam knew the reality. Emily Macklam was getting out, but not for any of those reasons, and not tonight; not Friday night, a night full of promise and one that was only just beginning.

At Nell's table, Emily had become fully engaged in re-telling the story of the 'southern twats' who had been unsuccessful in robbing Pettigrew's Hardware and Building Supplies. The general consensus among the girls was that if the villain with the broken foot made any attempt to sue Emily for her part in the capture of the two robbers, then they would find out where he lived and set fire to his house.

With that particular problem solved, they then moved on to the antics of one Peter Lewis, a person of interest, as the saga of his attempts to prise open the knickers of one Emily Macklam continued to run on monotonously. Janice Potter, one of the more outgoing but generally less worldly members of the group, recommended simple castration to solve the problem.

'If ye' cut a dogs nuts off like ... they dinnea' wan'te' shag any more de' they?'

It was an obvious question, with an equally obvious answer.

'So, A'h reckon we pop round his house like, wait

'til his missus goes out an' we'd only need four of us to hold him down like ... and then just cut his bloody nuts off!'

A searching look passed round the table. The worrying aspect appeared to be that Janice Potter was not joking. The questioning innocent expression on her face and laughter free eyes indicated she was totally serious so Nell voted to quickly change the subject.

'There's one or two right gadgie's in tonight ladies. Have yeez al' seen what's hangin' off the bar right now like?'

Seven heads turned in the direction of the bar. The place had begun filling up to the extent the young men fighting for attention from Tony the landlord and any one of his three overworked bar staff, were now standing two or three deep. The standard display offered varying views of flesh squeezing elastically tight jeans, recently purchased but made to look at least ten years old; small neatly packaged bum's and bared arms displaying a multitude of coloured tattoo's declaring undying love to someone called Alice, or alternatively someone else's Mum.

One tousle haired youth with a pint in each hand, and obviously searching for his best mate, caught the eye of Doris Blackwell, a long time member of the girls drinking group. He smiled. Doris and the distant stranger locked eyes. This young man had not been seen before in the Jolly Sailor and could well be considered as fresh meat. He appeared frozen to the spot as Doris dropped the front zip on her one piece dress a notch or two, providing a more than adequate view of the delights beneath. He began to mouth some words when a dyed blonde, short in stature and dressed to provide the maximum exposure of electrically tanned flesh appeared next to him. He had not immediately noticed her presence. His mind was elsewhere and obviously not too far from the bosoms of Doris Blackwell.

The short blonde stared long and hard at the youth and then turned her gaze on the subject of his blind attention ... Doris. She grabbed one of the pints her beau held a little unsteadily, took a substantial swig and then gave out her message.

'Divvin' gan' weighin' up maa' lad ye' skanky sod. If ye'eze clamming fe' sommat te' chew on like, they's a couple o' old men at the other end o' the bar Pet, a bit more your age like!'

The 'girls' laughed out loud; first conflict of the night now on the scoreboard. The angry blonde pulled the grinning, beer spilling red faced youth away from the bar, moving through the crowd until completely absorbed and out of sight.

The discussion fell back to default when Nell posed the obvious question: 'Where are we going tonight then girls?'

A few pubs and clubs were mentioned but the general consensus appeared to be they would probably end up at one of the dancing bars on the Marina. So, an hour or so of ear fracturing musical noise at the Jolly Sailor; a few pints at a couple of pubs down the road and then on to the serious business of the night, finding a sweet smelling body to press up against ... and maybe more!

The first two band members appeared at around eight thirty. They were middle aged, local, played country music quite well and all currently single. A busy Tony sent them over to sit with the girls and had two pints delivered ... on the house. This would not be the first drink they had downed that night and it definitely would not be the last. Unfortunately however, as the 'Rodeo Broncs' filled up with booze, their various musical skill sets would tend to deteriorate, to such an extent, that after an hour, everyone in the Jolly Sailor would be shouting for a more melodious rendering of out and out heavy metal.

Live music at the 'Jolly Sailor' was known more for quantity than quality. Tony the landlord had worked out the fine balance between booking acts with enough success and skill to attract new punters to his pub and booking regular not quite such accomplished musicians who would provide noise at high levels simply to drink to. The enthusiastic 'Broncs' fell into the second category and would be removed from the stage when things started to get broken.

Barry, the lead guitarist, stole a chair from somewhere and purposely sat between Emily and Nell. Out of the four 'Broncs', he was regarded as the biggest 'pain in the ass' and fancied Emily to the point of distraction. However, at twenty years older and a history with girls much younger than her, Emily offered no encouragement.

'So, how ye' doin' Pet?' the part time musician asked.

'Oh, as well as can be expected Barry. An' how about ye' like? Still employed ... or havin' a week off ... courtesy of the social like?'

'No Em, Ah've got me van have'nt A'h. A'h drive al' over the North East an' sometimes A'h do some trips te' Scotland like'

'Oh, good Barry. Ah'm right pleased fe' ye' Pet'

He pushed in a bit closer. Nell turned and gave Emily a knowing stare. Something had to be said.

'Did ye' have a little accident like, when ye' came out to'nite?'

'What de' ye' mean Pet?' Barry asked, slightly confused.

'Wi the bottle like ... the bottle o' midnight in Manchester ...?'

Barry could never be considered the sharpest knife in the block and had to ask again what Emily meant.

'A'h mean ye' stink like a Newcastle brothel keepers handbag Barry. D'ye think that smellin' like that will guarantee ye' a pull tonight like?'

Barry fell silent for a moment as seven more pairs of eyes focused on him, waiting for a reply, hopefully a witty reply, one that would test Emily's ability to strike back.

'A'hve never bin' te' a Newcastle brothel Em, so I wouldn't damn well know would I!' was the best he could do.

'Well, Ah'd think yee'd have a clue like when ye' walked in an' three females collapsed on the floor wi' chest complaints ... an' the young bar lad who brought ye pint over like, was wearing a gas mask ... did ye' no notice that Pet!'

It took a minute for the penny to drop.

'Oh, ye' mean the body splash Pet'

'The what?' Nell asked.

'The body splash! That's the latest thing Nell. Ah've got it on the internet like. It's a hormone thingy like they have in them very expensive Arab perfumes ... guaranteed to attract the ladies, like they do in them harems Nell!'

Conversation round the table had stopped; suppressed laughter hanging in the air. Nell gave Emily a look. They were both thinking the same thing.

'So ... what's the name o' this canny secret ingredient like, 'cause it looks as if it works Pet ... look how excited we all are round here?' Emily asked fascinated.

Providing backup ... the girls all nodded their heads vigorously, straight faced and showing a great deal of interest.

Barry now took on a look of slight superiority. The hours spent on the internet searching the subject of 'attracting women' appeared to be paying off.

'A'h think its called Musk ... or something like that Em ...!'

'Oh ... Musk, Barry. Ah'm not too sure like, but A'h think that comes from the arse of a deer Pet; they grab a deer an' then squeeze its arse, an whatever comes out of it, they call Musk'

Barry now looked confused once more.

'Are ye sure Em?' he asked.

'I am that Pet. We're sure arn't we girls ...?' she questioned as all the girls nodded in reply.

'So, let's get this absolutely straight like. Ye've got a stuff called body splash that ye' pour al' over ye' like ... an' in fact what ye've done is cover ye'sel in deer shit. Is that about it Pet?'

The spontaneous laughter from eight women literally cracking up turned every head in the Jolly Sailor. Barry however failed to see the depth of the matter and simply sat there, blissfully none the wiser. His band partner, sitting opposite, got the point straight away and hustled Barry to get up and head toward the small stage, hoping to explain the mystery of Musk and any improbable links to harems in Arabia on the way.

It was time for another round and a slightly

unsteady Tonia Biggs offered to do the honours. Although she was the youngest in the group there was no doubt she would be an experienced drinker by the time she reached twenty one ... if her liver didn't give up on her first.

The band, now assembled, began the process of tuning their instruments and agreeing the title of the opening number. The time it took would vary but the result would always be the same. The bass would end up playing a litte flat with the first number guarenteed to be a strange country styled version of Abba's Waterloo. The usual 'groupies' collected as near to the small stage as decorum would allow with the other three band members giving Barry as wide a berth as possible within the boundaries of the compact space.

A night of fun and possibly unknown adventure was about to begin.

Chapter Sixteen
9.00 pm

The girls had all agreed that when the 'Rodeo Broncs' announced 'Islands in the Sun' was to be their next number, it would be the signal to leave. There would be two overriding reasons. One; by the time 'Islands' came around in their running list, they would have been playing for over an hour. Two; groupie Elaine Withers would be invited to join Barry on the stage for the duet. Having to suffer one piss poor singer was bad enough, taking into account the price of a pint, but being subject to two at the same time could only be considered rude.

Tonia had nearly finished her beer from the last round and her eyes had begun to glaze over. It was quite possible that after just one more, she would be on 'remote control'. Through a slightly blurring vision and somewhat slower than normal ability to assess the good and the bad from the really ugly, young Tonia had locked onto a skinny youth propping up the bar with a couple of mates. If he was over eighteen, he didn't look it. He vaped annoyingly often, leaving a more or less permanent white cloud surrounding his head with people standing nearby waving their hands about in undisguised efforts to disperse the bothersome haze.

Emily had noticed the distant look on her friends face and made the connection with the spotty faced youth at the bar. She nudged Nell.

'A'h think our Tonia's bin' taken over by a beast from the planet Zog' she said quietly.

'Aye, it looks as if the skinny assed creature could well be a mixed race person wi a Ma from South Shields and a Da from one of the less salubrious parts of Zog ... an' probably on Universal Credit like!'

'She looks a bit worse for wear Nell, shall we get her in a taxi ... she may not last much longer ... an I certainly don't want her ending up wi' that pillock tonight?'

With a short discussion round the table, it was agreed that Tonia was more or less out of it. Nell rang for a taxi and ten minutes later Emily and Nell had managed to remove a well stoked eighteen year old Tonia from the packed and noisy venue to the relative quiet of the car park. Minutes later the taxi appeared and Tonia was safely on her way.

Emily checked her watch. It would be some quarter of an hour before 'Islands' would appear on the Rodeo Broncs running list and possibly time for another round. The two ladies made their way back inside the pub battling an elbow strewn path through the uncomfortably crowded bar area.

The spotty faced youth had been observing the removal of Tonia and as Emily squeezed past one of the two equally skin blemished youths he was standing with, the fatal words came forth.

'A'ha could get me hands round them tits like'

Nell, just in front of Emily, was on it immediately.

'What did ye say lad?' she asked quietly.

'A'h said .. ye canna land a job down the pits like ...! I were talkin' te' me mate here ... about work like, an' the fact there were none round here Pet ...'

The two accompanying stooges stood wearing a stupid grin; one to the Lions and none to the Christians.

'Howay man ... what would ye lot know about

work ... ye've never done any ... an it's the bloody money A'h pay every week ... te' thee government like, that pays for ye' bloody beer. So, if ye' make any more mistakes wi' words like tits and pits, ye can expect a quick disturbance to ye nappa like ... are ye' getting me Pet?'

'Who the hell d'ya think yeez' talkin' te' like .. yeez'll have me bubbling right fearsome in a minute ... won't she lads?

It was a brave move for someone who obviously had no knowledge of Nell's secret weapon, an object of regular but discreet discussion at the Jolly Sailor. Tony, the landlord, caught a snippet of the conversation. He had a pretty good idea how it would all end. He needed to get nearer to the action so he could intervene. Suddenly a space cleared around the youth and his two grinning companions.

Nell looked at Emily. It was about to happen.

'If I was you like, I'd be putting that beer down right now bonnie lad unless ye' want it al' over ye!' Emily warned.

How, man ... yeez' goin' aka like. Now ye' gi' away afor A'h clock ye' both one like ... an A'h hope ye' have ye' loyalty cards at A an' E wi' yer ... 'cause ye' goin' te' need em Pet ...!'

Too late! Surprise was to be the key. He would not be able to add any more to the bravely delivered comment, a bravery reinforced by ignorance, an ignorance that up to this point had been bliss.

Nell moved quickly sideways and backward grabbing the mouthy lad by the shoulders, pushing him hard against the bar. Her head snapped forward, so quick even the keenest of observers would have to pinch themselves that anything had actually happened at all. But it had ... and when Nell's forehead made a perfect connection with the bridge of the disrespectful youth's nose, the game was over. Nell let go of his shoulders. He sank to the floor screaming in a mixture of pain and embarrassment, his nose a bleeding mess. Emily grabbed Nell. She was now in full fighting mood looking to take on the two disbelieving mates of the fallen hero, both standing speechless with mouths open, finally realising everyone at the Jolly Sailor that night had known something they didn't.

A cheer went up from the girls table as Emily ushered a still tense Nell back to her seat. Tony, by this time had arrived to attend to the nearly unconscious blubbering youth with a damp bar cloth. Five minutes later with all three lads outside and away, the fun and frivolity for seven happy looking women and the hundred or so other punters in the Jolly Sailor that night could continue.

Friday nights were designed to forget the worries of the week, the month, the year and all the problems associated with survival in a fast moving twenty first century. The last thing Emily wanted to hear about in the Jolly Sailor was her brother Thomas, but that was not to be and when the tap on the shoulder came she looked up into the eyes of a young man; a complete stranger.

'Are ye' Emily Macklam wi' a brother Tom?'

'A'h maybe ... who are ye' like?'

'Ah'm Jimmy Little ... an' me brother's in the nick wi' Tom. He wa' only a passenger in the stolen car like. It were your Tom who stole it and was drivin' it. Me brother had nothin' te' do wi' it like ... and now the bobbies is blamin' im' ...'

The words tailed off. Emily turned in her seat to face the boy. He looked genuinely concerned. Nell had taken notice of the conversation, looking around to see if the lad was with anyone else, possibly a small team of young villains. No one else appeared to be hovering or paying the conversation any particular level of attention.

Emily took in the lad's features. He looked below drinking age, pale faced and probably poorly fed.

'A'h thought the other two in the car wi' Thomas were from the 'borough like'

'Well, me an' me Mam live here, but me brother lives wi' his Da in the 'borough'

'Well bonnie lad, why don't ye' Da or ye' Ma get im' out the nick like ...'

'They won't, they say they've had enough ... he'll have te' appear tomorrow ... wi' the others, wi' your Tom!'

'Well, Ah'm the same Pet. We've all had enough of these skanky kids. So now they'll have te' face up te' it all on their own. I'm doin' nout, me Ma's doing nout ... and me Da's pushin' up the bloody daisies ... so he's doing 'nout either.

The lad hovered. Whatever he expected from the sister of his brothers mate, this was not it.

'But ye've got te' help me ... will ye' come down the station wi' me an' talk to the rozzers like. It'll only take an hour ...'

'Look lad, ye' have te' understand these kids are goin' te' end up in prison for the best part o' their damn lives unless they get their act together now ... an' I mean ... right now!'

The lost looking lad stood there, not knowing what to do next.

Nell needed to end this conversation.

'OK. On ye' way now. Ye'll get nothing more from us an' ye' also look a bit young to be havin' a drink, so on ye' way lad!'

Giving out one final pleading look, the disappointed youth moved away from the table and pushed his way impatiently through the pressing crowd.

'A'h feel a bit sorry for im' Nell' offered Emily.

'There' no damn need to feel sorry for that lad Em. He's just one more of life's casualties, not for what he's done, or not done, but what his pissin' useless family is doing to him ... and the same damn thing is happening te' you. The sooner ye' get out o' this bloody comedy of horrors, the better. So ye' just concentrate on them soddin' certificates Pet 'caus they'ze ye' ticket outa' here!'

Emily thought on for a moment or two.

'Tell us a joke Nell and cheer us up for God's sake'

Nell was well known not only for her 'hands free' ability to floor young boys with a cheeky demeanour, she also had a genuinely deserved reputation for telling jokes. The table went quite.

'OK then ... but A'hm sure ye've heard this one before like'

'Oh c'mon Pet' shouted Doris Blackwell: 'Just get on wi' it!'

'Right. So this fella' walks in'te a bar like an' says te' the barman "Would ye' like to hear a funny joke about a Geordie my good man?"

The barman says: " Well ye' might like te' know Ah'm a Geordie, them two big fella's over there like, well they're Geordies; them two boxers in the corner ... well Ah'm afraid they're Geordies ... and that right hard looking towser at the end o' the bar is also a Geordie. So, me bonnie lad ... de ye' still wanna' tell us a joke about Geordies like?"

The fella puts his pint down and says wi' an air o' disappointment like: " Well not if Ah've got to tell it six bloody times!"

The table erupted. The gloom had gone. Emily Macklam had a smile on her face once more ... and the night was still young!

Chapter Seventeen
10.00 pm

With 'Islands' in full swing and a small group of swaying admirers squeezed in front of the stage, Nell announced to her 'team' it was time to go. The next alcoholic venue was only a short walk away. There would be no live music to disturb the serious matter of drinking at the Crown and Anchor and everything liquid between ten and twelve was on offer ... two for one.

Being too late for any form of seating, the girls pushed through to the end of the bar making for themselves a position that could be defended against others with a similar idea. Jeanie Stigwell shouted the round with pints following shots. The place was packed; the clientele a little older, mostly better dressed and generally better mannered than the Jolly Sailor. There were no fifteen year old 'bangers' in the car park or signs of fresh vomit indicating the entrance to the toilets.

This was a place where there was a much better chance of a 'pull' with someone who was hopefully employed, had his own wheels and preferably not living with his mum. It was a little early but within the hour the Crown and Anchor would be one squeezed and compacted chattering mass of bodies, all making purposeful contact with one another and checking to see if the heat of a likely encounter could perhaps be felt.

Emily had now begun to succumb to the effects of the beer and the first round of shots. Light in the room had taken on a definitive shimmer as natural hunting instinct took over. She felt taller, more attractive now and in need of something physical. Nell clocked the look, the searching eye, the wandering attention from the fascinating discussion being chaired by an equally inebriated Kylie Brooks.

'Well, A'h think yeez al' know me Ma and Da are not talking like ... an' it's getting right silly'

'What d'ye mean Kylie' asked an interested Nell.

'Well, they've bin writin' notes te' one another 'cause o' the not talking like. They're all over the bloody house ... stuck on cuboard's and left in shoes ... its bloody ridiculous'

'And ...?' Nell prompted. The girls were giving full attention except Emily who now looked to be in a distant place.

'Well, yesterday me Da wrote a note to me Ma to wake him up this morning at five o'clock like. He was on early shift an' had te go an' pick up me Uncle Jack ... te take im te work ... his car's knackered like!'

'So ...?'

'It were really funny. Me Da left the note on me Ma's bedside table, but when he woke up this mornin' ... it were nearly nine o'clock. He wa' right furious like until, as he wa' stormin' about the bedroom like, he spotted a note on HIS bedside table ... an it said "It's five o'clock ...WAKE UP Pet!" ...'

The whole gang burst out laughing except for Emily who had not really been listening and appeared to be practising telepathy with a swarthy looking, broad shouldered, slick haired young man several feet away down the bottom end of the bar. He looked as if he was on his own and chatting animatedly with a couple of obviously interested young girls. Emily clocked him to be around twenty-five'ish, or certainly less than thirty. He looked well dressed in a suit that had definitely not fallen off a peg or been stitched together by someone on piece-work in Yugoslavia.

Finally, the message got through. A lull in the conversation with the two girls gave him the opportunity to turn his head and immediately he locked on to Emily. He smiled exposing a bright, linear set of teeth and lifted his glass in Emily's direction. She raised her own in reply. The connection had been made; the conquest was to come.

Nell caught the action.

'Are ye' off over there Em?' she asked.

'Not yet Nell. This one's got te' come te' me!'

'Well, it must be your round then Pet' advised Nell through a smile.

The night's drinking continued at a pace for a group who steadfastly defended their place at the bottom of the bar, despite several attacks by small gangs of youths looking for a similar stronghold or young men who simply wanted to order more drinks.

'Ye'll have te' get taller or louder Pet!' Nell would shout when one attempted to push in.

'If ye want te' get taller, ye' can put some shit in ye' shoe like ... but if ye' want to get louder ye'll have te' grow a bigger chest than that. A'h can let ye' have a week o' two wi' me Charles Atlas expanders ... just look what they've done fe' me!'

At this point, Nell would pull back the top of her dress, exposing some lacy bra material and an expanse of smooth, scented flesh. Such a sight would normally claim the immediate attention of any errant red blooded male allowing Nell to gently push the distracted spectator away and back a step leaving the 'girls' fortress position at the bar intact.

Sometimes there would be a wise crack or two from the more sharper witted ones amongst them such as:

'Aye, wi ones like that, ye can make joggin' a spectator sport hinny! Where ye' runnin' on Sunday like?'

Emily, since making eye contact with the well groomed male, had ignored him, concentrating on the girl's continuous banter. Another one of Nell's jokes had been called for and with the amount of drink she now had inside her, she would be lucky if she could remember any.

'Right, I've got one for ye' ... are ye' ready?' she asked.

'Aye Nell' everyone shouted: 'Get on wi' it lass'

'Right then ...'

Nell cleared her throat, taking onboard another large intake of Cameron's Ruby red

'Well, this old girl ge's out te' the corner shop like. She asks the woman for a packet of Daz ... te' wash her budgie!'

A ripple of laughter.

'Hinney, A'h would'na recommend that like; it's a right powerful detergent pet ... an' it might kill ye' budgie like!

Howay man, said the 'ald girl. Me next door neighbour washes her budgie in Daz right regular, an' it comes up a treat!

Well, if ye' do wash ye' budgie in Daz ye' buy from me Pet, then ye' must take full responsibility ... dy'a see me point hinney?

So, a few weeks later the old girl comes inta' the shop again like. The woman asks how her budgie is. Oh, it's deed Pet ... completely deed.

A'h told ye the Daz would kill it like! The woman

said.

Oh no Pet, the old woman told her. It war'nt the Daz that did it ... it were when I put it through the mangle ...!'

They had heard the joke before, as they had most of Nell's comic repertoire but encouraged by the booze, and hyped up by the atmosphere everyone fell about laughing, as if they had heard it for the very first time. Emily was one of them, momentarily distracted from what else was going on around her.

Suddenly he was there, standing right beside her. Nell felt his presence also and looked as if she was moving into breast revelation mode, in order to protect the fortress. He directed his attention initially to Nell, then turned his head and caught the questioning eye of Emily.

Emily smelt him as he moved closer, now pressed up against her. It was a wonderful smell, an expensive smell and Hugo Boss appeared to be in the mix somewhere. He spoke first, talking to Nell but not taking his eyes from Emily.

'I hope you don't mind, I'm trying to find a way to the bar; I'm only getting one drink ... and then I'll be gone' he said.

Nell looked at Emily and then turned back to the girls. For her this was not a 'person of interest' ... Emily had gotten there first.

There was a slight accent in there somewhere.

'He must be a foreigner' Emily thought to herself: 'He speaks English too well!'

'Aye, if ye' squeeze ye trim little body in that gap there Pet, ye' can order as many drinks as ye' like ... like'

He smiled, revealing a close-up of a full set of George Clooney teeth. They could have been capped;

they could have been a complete stranger to any form of private dentistry whatsoever, but Emily considered whatever the 'root' of the matter, they looked magnificent ... so magnificent, Emily's gaze hung locked onto their brilliance for an embarrassingly long time.

He spoke again.

'So, can I come by then ... and get to the bar?'

The spell had been broken.

'Oh, of course Pet, help ye'sel like ... an' mine's a pint o' Cameron's Red Ruby!'

This generated yet another sparkling smile ... and the high levels of alcohol circulating throughout Emily's brain told her impetuously she was probably in full blown lust, or even slightly in lurve!'

Ye' not from round here like?' she questioned as the broad shouldered Adonis fought to hand over some money to an impatient barman.

'Your beer is on the bar ...' he indicated as he turned with a gin and tonic cupped protectively in both hands against possible spillage. She would have to repeat the question.

'Ye' not from round here like?'

'Oh ... well not really I suppose. I'm an engineer on the offshore wind turbine development. I train local engineers to maintain the generators. My normal home is Hamburg ... in Germany, but I travel a lot and will be here for another month or two'

'Oh ...' said Emily feigning some level of interest. It was too much information. All she wanted to know was that he wasn't some sort of terrorist, in town for a quick shag before going to blow something up. You had to be careful with foreigners!

'Well Pet, where are ye' livin' like ... whilst yeez' in town? Are ye' in a hotel or something?'

All she wanted to know was if he had a suitable place to go back to ... if his luck turned out to be 'in' that night of course. If not; if he was some sort of student living in skanky digs, or a flat share with other mates looking for a gang bang or even a married man who needed to pour his heart out before getting an erection ... then he would need to be dumped right now.

'I'm staying at the Premier Inn, up on the marina. My office is there also ... so it is very convenient'

Another smile! One thing was for sure, he damn well knew how to show off his very best points. The teeth had become slightly more than a fascination.

'D'ya have a name then Pet?

'Yes. My name is Helmut'

'Oh ... Helmet ... did ye' hear that Nell ... this good looking fella here is named HELMET ... now isn't that fantastic like. We've been searchin' for a good lookin' HELMET for some time ... haven't we Pet?'

'Aye, we have that Em ... helmet ye' say ... well, well, well ..'

'No, you have it wrong!' the broad shouldered German interrupted.

'It's HELMUT ... not HELMET ...'

The laughter erupting spontaneously from the corner of the bar caught the German unawares until Helmut clicked, and then he could do nothing other than join in.

Nell pointed to her watch, nearly eleven. Time to go!

'Goodbye Helmut' Emily shouted reaching for her pint and downing three quarters of it in just a few gulps, slamming the glass back down on the bar, a line of unattractive foam lingering on her lips.

'Thanks for the drink Pet. A'h may see ye' around

later like' and with that, arm in arm, Nell and Emily followed the other girls outside to a waiting taxi. The night so far had been good. All thoughts of a drunken mother and a completely delinquent brother forgotten; exasperation with an over sexed manager buried for the time being and having had an unexpected conversation with George Clooney's teeth, this experience would set the standard for what may yet lay ahead.

Chapter Eighteen
11.00 pm

The Marina area of town had been under development for some years. It was home not only to the general yachting community during the day, but the young movers and shakers at night. After ten thirty any spotter of Range Rovers, BMW's and Mercedes cars, most less than a few years old, would be in their element. This was where the young internet entrepreneur and EBay scam artist would show off his wares and Friday night was the time to pick up a little something for the weekend. So much for the tales of a derelict and disenfranchised North East then! Somebody had money; the people paying near London prices for a pint in all the outlets at the Marina must be making a living somewhere locally ... they couldn't all be driving up from the south just for a night out ... could they?

The area consisted of a collection of upmarket eateries and late opening music bars, conveniently supporting the development of a few hundred flats and apartments above, accessed by stairways between the various venues. After eleven, several bars would provide promotions designed to get women, of any age, in and drinking thereby providing a natural magnet to the entrepreneur on his quest to track down a little 'something for the weekend'.

The reputation was such that most bars and fast food eateries would be filling up at this time. There was not often trouble but now and again the odd fight between two rampant males over one goggle eyed female would break out and if for any reason it spread, then it would be every man for himself. The girls were not worried. Any individual, male or female, attempting to take on one of them would be taking on all of them. Anyone who regarded themselves as a regular weekend reveller in the Marina would know that and therefore such knowledgeable young men would normally give the group a wide birth.

The team's seven seat taxi dropped its giggling and vocally expressive cargo outside Georgio's, a bar serving drinks and fast food during the day and providing a moody, purposely dark atmosphere, along with some ear bending music, from eleven onward. Throwing out time would be around two or two thirty in the morning, depending on the number and possible fitness of any paying customers still remaining. The place was only half full when they arrived but people were coming in and out all the time. The girls were a well know group at Georgio's and not considered trouble makers unless someone was looking to break a particular reputation. They could all hold their drink well and always paid for their rounds unlike some of the other ladies groups that trawled the pavements of the Marina at a weekend.

Emily, with spirits lifted, set up a line of shots for the girls who were now in dancing mood. The ritual of placing handbags in the middle of the dance floor was not dead in the North East and served as a useful focal point for anyone whose head might be a little light.

The music volume, in such a relatively small space, would have been considered far too loud ... if any one of them had been sober. But no one was sober, so the deep bass notes and monotonous rhythms worked their magic, freely penetrating every nerve ending to combine with the near hypnotic violence of penetrating strobe lighting; designed to capture the very soul of just about everyone in Georgio's that night. She had a feeling the outing would go well as long as she managed to stay upright and Nell remained within close calling distance.

One bold young man appeared through the gloom and approached the girls. He looked relatively sober which was more than could be said for his dress sense. A white shirt opened nearly to the waist and trousers so tight they left literally nothing to the imagination confirmed whatever mission he was on that night was probably doomed to failure.

Nell, being the oldest of the group would answer the first question.

'Hi ladies ... A'h saw ye' over here like ... and A'h thought ye' might like a drink ... like!' he shouted.

'What ... all of us?' Nell questioned loudly.

'Aye, well ... that's ne' problem Pet. A'h can handle it. What'll it be?'

'Well, where d'ya keep al' ye money like ... in tight kek's like that lad?' Emily asked, the others now showing definite signs of interest with all eyes momentarily focused on a small bulge in the rather bold stranger's pocket area.

He looked down, one hand instinctively falling to protectively cover the small lump.

'Well A'h ...'

The young man was showing signs of confusion. Nell followed up.

'A'hm afraid we'll have te' refuse ye' like ... won't we girls?'

A violent nodding of heads.

'Ye see lad ... if that's all ye've got like ... it won't

be enough to serve all of us ... will it Em?'

'Oh no Nell ... unless he's got some change shoved away somewhere, in a place we can't see like!'

The girls all remained stone faced ... nodding heads in agreement.

'Oh ... right then ... Aye, well then ... perhaps I'd better be getting back te' me mates like ...'

'Aye, that'll be right canny Pet' agreed Nell as the young man with no dress sense disappeared back into the pulsating gloom.

Time for another round!

It would be several minutes later, when her drink had not been touched, that anyone thought to ask where Kylie Brooks was. She had been fully present when the conversation with 'tight trousers' had taken place, but now she was not immediately visible. Protective Nell and her close shadow Emily went on the hunt. Kylie had only recently split up from a partner who after six months of dodging the subject of his home address, and demanding sex in the most unusual places, had finally admitted he was married and lived happily with a wife and young child in Peterlee.

It had set Kylie back somewhat, making her prone to going off on her own in a moody fit, leaving her vulnerable to any of the various two legged preying monsters known to inhabit the darker areas of the Marina.

The pavement space outside of Georgio's had been filled with about a dozen or so timber tables and bench seating. They had found the missing Kylie and accompanying her, with hand outstretched across the table, was her ex-boyfriend Johnnie, the man from Peterlee.

He spotted Nell and Emily approaching and

quickly withdrew the hand. Kyle turned her head.

'It's OK Nell' she said: 'Johnnie an' me is just havin' a little chat ... that's all. We wa' goin' for a walk round the Marina in a minute like. I'll be in later'

Johnnie held a self satisfied look on his face as if to say 'You see ... I got her ... and I can just pick up where I left off at any time I please'

Emily sensed the situation could get messy. She looked to Nell for some indication of what might happen next. Her face had become dark, the hard shadows underlining her mood. His became suddenly pale, taking on the complexion of an un-fried chip.

'Well, A'h think ye' should just come inside Pet an' join the rest o' us like. This piece o' shit is only trouble ... wi' a capital tee like'

'A'h don't like ye' talking like that Nell. That's right rude man ... so now A'h think ye'd better piss off like!'

'A'hm not talkin te ye' ... ye divvy bastard'

He was sitting down and Nell was standing up. He knew Nell's reputation. The odds were against him whilst he was sort of locked into the wooden seating unit. He needed to stand up to have any kind of a chance.

Kylie, although suffering from the effects of substantial inebriation felt it her duty to intervene.

'Ohhh ... Nell Pet; there's ne' need te' talk te' our Johnnie like that, he's only ...'

'Our Johnnie is it now lass? This is the shit that shagged ye' senseless for bloody months on end an' then told ye' he wa' married ... an' wi' a baby bairn te' boot like!'

The errant and rueful Johnnie looked to make a move, up and out from the confines of the pick-nick table arrangement he was momentarily restrained by.

'Don't even think o' moving lad. If anyone's going te' walk away from this table, its goin' te' be Kylie ... not you. There's still a chance ye'll be leaving horizontal like ... if ye' want te' avoid that ... stay where ye' are!'

People nearby were now taking notice; the background conversations fading away with everyone's attention drawn to the unfolding episode of a Cleveland version of Eastenders.

'So, Ah'll ask ye' again Kylie ... will ye' no drop this bloody wanker an' come wi' us. A'hm tellin' ye' now, if ye' leave here wi' him ... and you in this damn state, he'll have the knickers off ye' in minutes like ... an' up against the nearest bloody dustbin. Is that what ye' want fe' yersel' tonight ... is it?'

Kylie's eyes began to well. Tears would fall within seconds. A voice, a male voice and someone who obviously knew the lacklustre male looking for an escape route, shouted out quite bravely: 'Gi' her a clout Johnnie ... gi' her a bloody clout man!'

Without turning Nell answered with: 'De ye' na' worry bonnie lad; when Ah've fixed this skinny toe rag ... Ah'll be back there looking for ye' like!'

Johnnie could see the determination in her eye. Nell could sense that 'flight or fight' was probably the only question devouring the limited thought processes of the young man, trapped where he sat by the restrictive timber construction.

'Em, why don't ye' go and give Kylie a hand like. She can come inside wi' us ... an' leave this pile o' shite te' go an' find himself another vacant bucket te' go an' piss in ...'

Kylie, now in full flood, allowed herself to be gently levered out from the table. Her handbag however remained in the middle of the tabletop and as Emily went to retrieve it, the angry youth grabbed at it, a thin smile emphasising the triumphant look of revolt. It took only milliseconds for Emily to process the situation, grabbing Kylie's half empty beer bottle, only inches away, and smashing the base of it on the table.

Johnnie didn't need a script to tell him what might be coming next. These two women were obviously out of their damn minds and if he didn't make the right decision and make it quickly, he would definitely be in some need of the infamous loyalty card for A & E.

He made his move. It was fumbling and inelegant causing a slight increase in the whisper level from the intensely interested audience.

'Howay man!' Nell shouted as a mumbling defiant Johnnie shuffled off, threatening to come back and 'do yer!' as he put it.

Nell turned to face the crowd of observers.

'Now then ... where's that big mouth bastard who wanted te' gi' me a clout like?'

With the three girls back inside; Kylie shoved in front of her drink and Nell calmed down enough to want to tell the story, Emily checked her watch. Perhaps, with the witching hour approaching, it would be time to go home. Suddenly, the night had lost its lustre. However, there was still Nell's telling of the events outside to listen to and no doubt with a bit of embellishment and a few amusing similes to add a certain flavour to the tale, this could end up being the highlight of the night.

A gentle touch of the arm came from behind. Emily looked round. With all the scattered strobe lighting momentarily spoiling her focus, she turned completely to confront whoever it was who had touched her.

'Wie geht's ...' offered Helmut.

Emily smiled.

'Well hello my little German friend ... what ye' doin' here like? Ye' not followin' me are ye?'

'No ... I'm not following you. I just thought it would be good if I could buy you a drink ... you would actually finish'

Suddenly her life had changed. The lovely Helmut was here and maybe there was more promise in this particular Friday night than Emily had thought not less than a few minutes ago.

Chapter Nineteen
Midnight

The girls all provided Helmut with a suitable greeting as Emily pushed him forward into the centre of the group, testing his mettle and possibly his sense of humour. Emily knew why he was there and Helmut knew why he was there but the others hadn't quite latched on yet, except Nell, who had a plan in case the one Emily had obviously been working on fell flat.

It was a dangerous time to be joining this particular crowd of women; dangerous for two reasons. For example, if any one of them managed to get themselves into a possible altercation, then the rest of the 'gang' would be expected to join in ... and if he was with them then it would also include him. The other danger of course would be the advertising of his affections for anyone other than the young lady who had invited him to join the group. Wandering eyes were not suffered under 'girl's night out' rules and this might be a little difficult to explain to someone who's first language was not English and certainly not Geordie English.

True to his word, he bought a round of drinks and immediately gained the affectionate tag of 'Helmut with the Helmet'. Janice Potter felt it necessary to sniff him; she categorised all of her men by smell, whilst Doris Blackwell was more interested in what might be filling his pants. Emily knew the best way to handle the situation was to let them all loose and get the necessary drunken comments and lewd remarks out of the way so she could perhaps hold a conversation with the man; the man who even looked good in the unflattering glare of disco lights.

The music could be considered generally too loud, the dance floor too crowded, the drinks service too slow and the heavy aroma of illegal tobacco products filling the air close to eye watering. However, for Helmut and Emily it was as if they were cosseted in a small packet of space insulated from all that was going on around them. Emily wanted to know more about this interesting looking man.

'So Pet' she offered, as the interrogation process conducted by 'les girls' came to a faltering end ... and their attention became diverted elsewhere: 'What can ye' tell me about ye'sel like?'

'What do you want to know?' replied a confident German.

'Well, are ye' married, have ye' any kids hidden away somewhere, are ye' fully employed and do ye' have any sexually transmitted diseases?'

Helmut considered the question for a moment.

'No ... err ... no ... err ... yes and definitely no!'

'Well that's a good start like'

Emily was warming to this man with a quiet, confident personality, intelligent eyes and an expensive smell.

'So, how is it a good lookin' fella like you's not married like. Ah'd ha' thought with al' those firm figured blond lassies like, over there in Germany, you'd be spoilt for choice Pet?'

Was this just small talk or was there a plan, a meaning to the questions Helmut wondered. They both knew how the night would end. Even though this extremely good looking young lady had consumed a few drinks throughout the night, she appeared to be in full control of her faculties and there had been a spark between them the first time they touched, back in the Pub. Patience would be required to tempt Emily Macklam into the broad and comfortable bed taking up space in room 114 at the nearby Premier Inn; a place close enough to walk to or stagger to, depending upon a particular state of mind.

'Let's have a dance' she declared, grabbing hold of his jacket sleeve.

Pushing outward, finding a space, Emily laid her arms across the shoulders of her captive German and began rotating her hips to the mixed musical rhythms, pushing gently into him. He took the intimate move to be a sign of approval of everything that had taken place between them so far.

Nell had found herself a guy to drape herself over whilst moving around the dance floor, bumping into just about everybody and not giving a damn. After the recent debacle outside, everyone with any sense would be giving them a wide berth.

'Is that girl a long time friend of yours?' he asked as Nell and her inebriated dance partner bumped into them for the tenth time.

'She is wi'out doubt me very best friend in al' the damn world like' Emily quickly replied.

'Ye' see, A'h have a few problems at home like, wi me brother and me mother ... an Nell helps me cope wi' it all. She's there when A'h need her Pet ... and that what good mates are for like!'

'Well, I can see you are both close. Do you do everything together?'

Emily thought about that for a second or two, unaware of where the conversation might be going.

'Aye, we do most things together like. Surely you've got a mate, a best mate that ye' do things wi' in

Germany Pet. Everyone needs somebody they can trust like, someone te' confide in, tell al' their troubles te' no matter what ...'

'Yes, I suppose I have someone like that, a guy I went to University with in Hamburg. He and I go out a lot when I'm at home. We have had some good times together ... in fact he will coming over to England to stay with me for a week very shortly. We are going to drive around and visit a few places. He would probably get on very well with your Nell'

There were no alarm bells, no warning signs. The conversation would simply lead on to it.

Emily wanted to know if the attractive foreigner held more potential than possibly a few hours of smooth sex.

'So, can ye' earn a good wack bein' an engineer wi' the turbines like? Ah've heard them guys as works offshore get right good money ... an' a lot o' em' come to this town to spend it'

Helmut was not shy about revealing how he made his living or how much he collected in his bank account for doing so.

'I can earn eighty to ninety thousand Euro's in a good year and then there is all other kinds of allowances for me to work here ... in Britain'

'Sort'a like a hardship allowance Pet?'

'No. Not a hardship allowance. It is no hardship working here and spending nights with someone as gorgeous as you Emily'

The complement took her by surprise.

'An ye've no long term partner in Germany ... no one ye've an' attachment to like; someone waiting for ye' when ye' get back te' Hamburg ... ?'

'No. I'm free and single. For the past several years I have been dedicated to education, driven by parents who only want the best for me. However, that has meant spending three years at University and then a further three years training as an engineer. So with all that behind me and fortunate to have a good job I enjoy, I'm now free to just have a good time'

'Well, that's cracking Pet. A'h admire ambition in a man and A'h reckon, as they say around here, the cut of ye' jib suits me fine, right fine like'

She pushed into him a little harder, feeling a movement, a firmness, an indication of possible excitement ahead.

'And what about your friend Nell, the person you like to do things with. Do you think she will going home with her dancing guy tonight ... or perhaps have something else on her mind?'

Emily had not caught on.

'No Pet, A'h don't think she'll be goin' home wi' that tit. A'h mean, I suppose she'll stay wi' us like, ye' know, all of us, all of us girls like!'

'But maybe she would like to stay with us, for the rest of the night perhaps?'

'Oh, she will that Pet. A'hve told ye', she will stay wi' us like, all us girls, an if ye' want te' tag along, yeez' welcome like'

Even in the disturbing light of the dance floor Helmut's face would show a particular level of frustration. He would have to come straight out with it and take the risk.

'What I really meant was, would your friend Nell like to come and join us, you and me, back at my hotel room ... the three of us?'

Alarm bells rang; had an unexpectedly mischievous spirit been inserted into the conversation? Had this smartly presented German inherited a British sense of humour somewhere along the way?

The anticipatory look on his face denied breathing room to such positive theories.

The penny finally dropped. It must have been the booze as Emily would normally have been way ahead of the kind of conversation she had been having for the past several minutes with this obviously unpredictable European. Had it all been leading to this; a gruesome threesome, in a bare arsed room ... in a travelling salesman's hotel.

Emily showed no sign of her anger or in fact her disappointment. She thought her rather pleasant looking admirer was better that this.

Well here goes ...

'Nell Pet ... Helmut wi' the helmet has asked me te' ask ye' if ye' would like to join him an' me in his room at the Premier Inn like? What de' ye' think ...?'

Nell turned to face the hopeful, expectant looking and deliciously smelling young man. Helmut thought she was perhaps considering what he regarded as this excellent offer. He smiled hoping it looked encouraging. She smiled back, a thin wide grin hiding her disbelief. Emily raised creased eyebrows in apprehension, having more than a small idea of what was to come next.

'So Helmut ... yeez' lookin' fe' a three's up like an' it seems by some stroke o' good fortune, yeez' chosen us like!'

He continued to smile. He was perfectly at ease with himself. It appeared things were going to go his way. It looked as if he was about to get a resounding 'Yes'!

'Well, ye' see, me Ma often told me ye' can always judge a man by his underwear ... namely, is he wearin' any ... or not!'

By this time, the other girls had realised something was going on. The conversation amongst them died as one by one they locked into Nell and Helmut. They moved closer to him, securing the perimeter. It was turning into an uncomfortable situation.

'So, tell me Helmut wi the Helmet ... are ye wearing any undies like?'

A hand snaked out from somewhere, searched for and quickly found its soft but stirring target. The hand belonged to Doris Blackwell and the target belonged to the nervous German. She squeezed hard and he let out what can only be described as a 'muffled scream' attempting to bend forward but hindered by the group of determined, unsmiling women packed tight into him.

'No Nell ... A'h don't think he's wearing any ... A'h think he's out dressed full Commando tonight like! Perhaps he wa' expecting a quick conquest behind the dustbins ... perhaps that would be you Em?' Doris confirmed.

'Oh no Doris ... his idea is te' have me an' Nell on one of them big ald' beds in the Premier Inn like'

'Well I'd be quite happy te' ... wouldn't ye' Pet ... as long as his plonker is big enough like!'

'Well, let's have a look!' said Emily.

Seven inebriated and therefore inhibition-less women grabbed the now very anxious looking young man, someone obviously searching for more than one fully attentive northern lass to spend the rest of the night with.

It took only seconds, his trousers lowered, ripped at a seam and down by his ankles. Doris Blackwell's first assessment appeared to be correct ... Helmut with the Helmet was not wearing any 'undies'.

Out came mobile phones, not only from the

group but also other interested nearby patrons. Nell and the girls moved away. Without their support, and his trousers by his ankles, the humiliated German could do nothing other than fall over, fully exposing his unfortunately unspectacular reproduction equipment. Helmut with the Helmet did not live up to expectations.

Nell made an announcement to the room.

'This geet' wazzock ha' come up here al' the way from Germany like, te find hi'self two lovely lookin' young ladies an' have a double-up at the Premier ... free o'charge ... it won't cost ye' a penny girls. Is there any of ye' volunteerin' like?

'Tie im up!' shouted someone.

'Piss on im!' shouted another.

Emily looked down on the unfortunate Helmut.

'What a shame lad. We might have had a nice night like, even in a bloody Premier Inn. But, we've asked around Pet ... as ye' can see ... and no one wants te' do a double up wi' ye like ... so we think it would be best if ye' gathered ye skanky kecks, git' down on ye' honkas like an make a quick bloody exit!'

The flashes of camera phones followed a thoroughly humiliated Helmut out the door on all fours as the girls turned to attend to more serious matters, such as who's round it damn well was?

Was this failed attempt to lure two semi-inebriated and attractive northern girls to room 114 at the nearby Premier Inn to be the peak of the evening's entertainment? Emily wanted to stay out for longer but not for so long she would end up in the despairing company of a bunch of drunken women all with tales of woe to tell as they studied yet one more insipid pastel sunrise.

Her mood right now was good and lifted in one way by the amusing outcome of the Helmut situation but lowered in another knowing she had now to put the possibility of a more positive physical encounter behind her. Unless her luck changed in a more acceptable direction, Justin Bieber would be required to do a lot more than play around with his underwear. Her attention was drawn back to the 'gang'. It looked as if another round would shortly be on its way.

Someone shouted it was close to one o'clock and the bar would be closing soon. This resulted in yells of disappointment and the expected run of fresh drinks orders. Emily, still musing at the outcome of her unfulfilled connection with Helmut the German decided to take some air and fill a seat in the pavement area. It was half empty now and a pleasant evening with cars regularly passing by looking for parking places. All she wanted was to be away from the noise and chatter inside the bar for a minute or two and just nurse her drink with unwelcome thoughts of facing the next day at home attempting to invade her current unsettled peace.

Chapter Twenty
1.00 am

Doris Blackwell had recently celebrated her twentieth birthday, if calling a three hour lunchtime session in the Jolly Sailor a celebration. Like Emily, she suffered from a demanding home life and a particular desperation to get out from under.

Doris had no plan. She had little or no regularity in her life other than the guaranteed Friday night out with the girls. She was as bright as a button but lacked any real form of ambition. She knew of Emily's plans. Everyone in the group knew of Emily's plans to take London by storm and Doris considered if she looked half as good as Emily, with or without makeup, she would probably have wanted to join her. But she didn't, and so that was that. There could be no half measures. Emily was a clever kid as far as Doris was concerned. She had lots of front, was well put together and possessed ambition in spades. Going to London was the right thing for her ... but not for everyone.

She stood at the door to Georgio's thinking of having a seat outside and taking in a bit of fresh air. She spotted Emily and walked over to sit beside her.

Doris, someone with an unfortunately old fashioned name she didn't like, had spent all her life in the North East. She came from a mining family but her father was still alive. She suffered from being the eldest of four children, individuals who took second place to her mother's busy social life and her father's addiction to the success and welfare of the local social club, of which he was secretary.

She worked at Tesco's and had done since leaving school. Her two younger brothers and one younger sister were a constant problem regularly acting out some ingeniously constructed attention-getting event that fell on deaf ears as far as their parents were concerned.

'How's it goin' Em' she asked.

Emily looked up, shaking herself out of her depressive thought mode.

'It's OK Dor ... it's OK A'h suppose'

'A'hm sorry about Herman the German Em ... he looked quite nice really'

'A'h know Pet. To be truthful A'h wa' lookin' for a good rough an' tumble te'night like ... but he went an' spoilt it all by being greedy ...!'

Both girls laughed.

'How's it goin' at work ... A'h mean how's it really goin wi that dickhead Lewis? Is he still tryin' that bloody hard te' get inside ye' knickers like?'

'Aye Doris. There's ne' stopping him. He came very near to gettin' a clout t'day not only from me, but from Billy as well. He wa' furious when he saw the claggy bastard try an' corner me outside the toilet like. A'h really don't want Billy te' get involved. He needs his damn job even though he's got te' work for the company asshole. Me, A'hm goin' te' be gone when A'h get me certificates like, so A'hm not too worried Dor ... but it is a difficult situation ... especially wi' all the pressure at home!'

Doris extended a hand across the table and caught Emily's.

'Don't worry Pet ... as me Ma al'ways says ... it'll all come out in the wash ... whatever the hell that's supposed te' mean'

'But what about you Dor' Emily asked: 'How's things wi' ye' parents like. D'ye even see em' at all?'

'No, not really Em. As ye know, since the pit closed an' me Da's bin out o' work his whole bloody life is spent in the club. He's now talkin' about settin' up a pigeon hospital ... d'ye hear that Em ... a bloody pigeon hospital in our garden shed. He's gone aka like, completely off his bloody head. An' me Ma, who only had one night a week free due to her social commitments to all the damn committees she sits on, has now filled that up wi' some sort o' charity night te' help them Syrian refugees. I tell'ed her like, it's na' they bloody Arabs ye need te think about ... it's ye' own damned kids running wild al'over the place like and causin' bloody havoc!'

Emily nodded her head; taking another mouthful of her Vodka and Tonic. She knew Doris' parents. She had been for a drink now and again with the girls at the club her father claimed more-or-less as his own. What was it that made him so dedicated to the job, the unpaid and unheralded work he carried out each day, spending literally every waking hour in the damn place? It certainly wasn't the cheap booze; he hardly drank. It certainly couldn't have been the accolades; he received more complaints than praise from the regularly unsatisfied members who wanted more bang for their annual 'buck', the 'subs' paid by the members to keep the place open.

However, except for perhaps the threat of an all out nuclear war, James Albert Blackwell would continue to spend every waking hour at the club as he had done for so many years past. Therefore as far as his kids were concerned, it was someone else's problem ... it was something a woman did ... looking after kids! It was not a man's problem until one of them needed a solid clip round the ear. There were women in the household ... it was their problem.

Her mother, a firm figured and physically attractive fifty something, spent her daytime energies scouring charity shops for the latest size ten fashions with matching shoes and handbag. She had connections with all the shop managers and sat on local committees of one or two of them. They would ring her when something really good came in and she would jump in her ten year old Ford Fiesta, often breaking what she considered to be unnecessary speed limits in order to make sure she had first refusal.

'At least ye' Ma manages te' speak a few words te' ye' durin' the week like. Mine is mostly too pissed to communicate wi anything other than the bottom of a whiskey bottle Dor. But there's no doubt that lad of ours, Thomas; well he's goin te' prison ... A'hm sure of it. In some ways, it'd be better if he did and then A'h could get on wi' my life Dor. As long as he's like he is ... and getting away wi' it like, then the coppers are gonna' continue te' keep putting pressure on me!'

'Well' offered Doris: 'This is the life up here Pet. There's nay money, nay jobs worth a shite an' all the government hand out's goin' te the bloody southerners, and it's not in our bloody pockets Em ... it's a damned disgrace A'h tell ye' ... a damned disgrace!'

'That's why A'hm gettin' on me bike and goin' down there te' join em Dor ... get me hand on some o' them handouts and get me'sel a bloody decent job!'

'What'll ye' do if it don't work out like ... if ye' can't get a job ... ye know ... cause ye' from the north like. I hear they just don't like us down there Pet an' it seems they can tell where ye' from as soon as ye' open ye' mouth Em!'

They both laughed out loud.

'Don't be so bloody daft Dor ... we al' speak English don't we and A'h speak it perfectly ...!'

'Well, when ye' get down there, ye'll have te' learn a new language like. There'll be no pints o' 'heavy' in pubs ... that is if ye' can afford te' actually buy a pint of anything down there wi' them London prices. Ye won't be able te' call someone a 'wazzock' as it might be insultin' some tribe or other from the African desert ... an one o' them might just be sittin' next te' ye' like'

Emily smiled. Doris Blackwell was a tonic; just the tonic she needed and now she was in full flight.

'I've heard Pet that when ye' go out wi' boys down there, as soon as ye' speak an' give away ye' from the north, when they take ye' back te' their place, they expect ye to do the washin-up a'for ye have a shag like!'

'I really don't think it's like that Dor' interrupted Emily, holding back tears of laughter.

'No Em it is ... it really is like' stated her straight faced friend; 'An' I've heard that unless ye've been te' Uni' at Oxford and posh places like that ... then ye' can't drive a car in the middle of London wi'out payin' money te' the Mayor .. an' that's a fact Em!'

'A'h think that's pushing it Dor'

'No Em ... A'h know for sure, it's to stop all the good shops on that Oxford Street cloggin' up wi' refugees and foreigners an' they gi' it a name like. They call it the education charge or somethin' and there's signs up everywhere like!'

Emily was forced to give the matter slightly more than a second's thought and then the damn bell rang.

'Ye daft cow, that's the bloody 'congestion' charge ... not an 'education' charge ...!'

With laughter echoing round the emptying Marina frontage, Emily felt in a mood several shades better than she had when Doris decided to join her. A spontaneous hug confirmed they both felt the same.

Deciding on whether to have another drink or not and if so would it be a pint or something a little more elegant, Emily and Doris took only casual notice as a large white, eighteen plated BMW pulled up in a space right outside Georgio's. Two casually dressed guys got out; late twenties, early thirties and looked around. They were on a mission.

They spotted the two girls sitting on the wooden bench seating, chatting away, engrossed in themselves and generally ignoring everything else going on around them.

This would not do.

They sauntered over to the table.

There were two spare seats.

The words came in a practised, near professional manner and would not be the first time they had been used as an opening line that night

'Hi ladies ... can we buy ye' a drink like?'

Emily and Doris stopped talking, both looking up at the two young men with a BMW standing at their table. The first measure had to be shoes. If the shoes were of good quality, in fashion, clean, polished and well maintained, then that could be a starter for ten.

They looked down. The result was satisfactory.

The second measure moved up a foot or so; trousers or jeans?

Both wore trousers, tightly tailored and perhaps a little too close a fit in the crotch area leaving little to the imagination. The shirts were colourful, well cut to a particular body fit and looked expensively made.

Emily checked her watch confirming time was

slipping away at a few minutes before two. She caught the eye of Doris who nodded her head. Could these two young men, whose most attractive feature so far had been the BMW, be on a promise?

Well, another drink and a short conversation would soon settle the matter!

Chapter Twenty One
2.00 am

The two young men hovered, waiting for a reply from the two ladies at the table, one regarded by both as very 'fit' looking and the other in a slightly different league. The 'lads' with the big BMW were after one thing and one thing only that night and all four individuals knew what that was. However, before such an outcome could possibility could be discussed, an investment would need to be made in a round of drinks. The two hopefuls would go to the bar together in order to decide 'who' was to eventually have 'who', as if the decision would actually be theirs to make. However, this provided a little space for the 'girls' to decide whether or not they would simply take the drinks ... and then tell the two 'chavs' to piss off.

To impress the young men and make sure they had a 'drink worthy' glass in front of them whilst the inevitable verbal sparring took place, both Emily and Doris had ordered a long Classic Mojito costing the expectant couple close to ten quid each. They had a smile on their faces when they delivered them and had obviously agreed 'who' was to have 'who' with the taller, leaner version and BMW driver placing himself on the bench next to Emily.

Now he was close, she could smell him. She couldn't put a name to it. It was a 'not unpleasant' aroma but also not an expensive one. The flash car could be borrowed, a company vehicle or mortgaged up to the eyeballs, so made no statement to Emily about the man except for the fact he had the keys to it in his pocket. Lots of options circulated her mind. On the one hand her body told her she needed an event that particular night, an event that would leave her breathless and drained, perhaps even wanting more from whoever it was she would end up clinging too afterward. Was this young man it? Perhaps yes and perhaps no but one thing was for sure, she did not need a long conversation about it. The matter was becoming pressing ... increasing in urgency with every drink.

The other stockier male sat next to Doris making sure he left some acceptable space between them. He appeared reserved to the point of shyness and unless he was hiding some fiery amorous character that would suddenly come to life as Doris passed a caressing hand over his thigh, then this competitor for her favours would probably miss out in the short term. However, Doris was a good talker and regarded her new companion as a challenge.

Emily and Doris passed a look of 'so far so good' between them and now the trial would begin.

The lean one introduced himself as Tyrone ... but call me 'Ty' and the stockier one revealed his name to be Amjad.

'Are ye related like?' Emily asked.

'No' replied Ty: 'We work together, in the same firm like'

'Oh ... an' what firm's that Pet?'

'It's a utility company and we're both sales advisors ...'

'Top sales advisors!' emphasised Amjad triumphantly.

'Oh, well that's nice' added Doris, hopefully putting an end to the pleasantries: 'So, what ye' doin' out tonight like ... are ye' from round here yous' two?'

'Aye ... we share a flat together, up near the ... err ... up near the headland'

Amjad looked as if he was about to add another emphasis or correction to what Tyson had just said, but then appeared to think better of it.

'Well, that's funny. As soon as A'h saw ye's like A'h said te' Em here, A'h said, them twos getting out the car like ... A'h reckon they share a place together ... probably quite a nice place like; I said that didn't A'h Em?'

'Yes ye' did Dor ... ye' certainly did ...'

Doris wore her fixed smile; her dumb looking fixed smile. She was having a game and Emily, having nothing else to do and nowhere else to go, thought it would be good to play along.

After a short Hollywood pause Tyrone continued to probe further.

'Are ye ladies livin' in a flat like, are ye ...'

'No Darlin' interrupted Doris: 'We're both homely girls like. There's ten of us at my house Pet and nine at Em's. A'h can tell ye it's a bit o' a struggle like fitting ten in two small rooms an' me Ma and Da on the social like. A'hm only allowed out once a week ... an Em's pretty much the same ... arn't ye' Em?'

'Aye Dor ... that's a fact like!'

'We just wanna' get away from it all Pet ... find a fella' wi' a nice apartment like, just the kind o' thing youse two lads have, ye know, a nice quiet place te' just call home. That's what we're lookin' for isn't it Em ... isn't it really ...?'

'Aye Dor ... that would be perfect Pet!'

Amjad had begun to look a little nervous and fidgeted to add another inch or so of space between him and Doris. A rather less concerned Tyrone asked a question, looking at Emily.

'So, do you two lovely ladies have a name?'

'Oh yes Pet. I'm Emily and my friend here is called Doris'

'Well now, Doris is it ... Doris who bunks in wi' nine others in a two room flat. Well Doris, let me congratulate ye' for being so honest about ye' situation and of course there'll be no problem with you moving in wi' us will there Amjad ... but it will have te' be after the weekend like as we've got a couple of Arab refugees wi' us at the moment ... an' they're not leavin' 'till Monday!'

The girls burst out into unrestrained laughter; Tyrone smiled the broadest of smiles and Amjad sat with a confused look on his face waiting for someone to explain what had just gone on.

'Well, it's really nice te meet ye' two great lookin' girls and A'h can see ye' both have a sense o' humour ...' Tyrone continued.

'Don't get too slushy Pet. Let's just leave it at 'great lookin' and say thanks for the drinks'

'So, unless ye' don't want te' tell us like, what do ye' do for a livin'?'

'A'h work in a hardware shop and Doris works in Asda's ... and both of us live at home. We're wi' a gang of girls like ... who're inside an' we'll be getting a taxi home in case ye' need te' ask the question. Is that OK like, is that what ye' wanted te' hear like?'

The sparring had begun.

'That's fine Emily. There's no doubt in me mind that you an' me will be making fantastic love before this night is out an ...'

'Night's gone already' interjected Doris: 'It's tomorrow mornin' now man and neither of us want to be caught havin' sex in broad daylight ... do we Pet?!'

Emily laughed.

'Speak fe' ye'sel Dor, I quite like seeing what A'hm gettin' me hands round, so broad daylight suits me Pet. Don't forget what our Nell says, ye can always judge a man by his underwear an' ye can't see much of it in the dark ... can ye'?'

Amjad continued looking confused and seemingly detached from the banter.

'An' what about you Ty, what kind o' underwear would an adventurous young lady discover if ye' dropped ye' strides in front of her right now like?'

Emily dropped her hand beneath the table to rest on her thigh, waiting for a reply from Tyson who was beginning to look a more and more attractive proposition as the minutes ticked by. She hoped he would not say the word 'commando' because if he did then his luck would definitely be out for now and any foreseeable time in the future.

'I'm a boxer shorts man me'sel like. A'h need a bit o' room in me underwear te' let things move around a bit Pet'

It was the right answer and Emily's hand moved across the bench and onto the thigh of the eye-catching BMW driver, feeling him flinch slightly at the first touch. She caught his eye, he remained tense as her hand wandered; searching for what she hoped would be a sizeable handful. Something was moving. What Tyson had tucked into his boxer shorts held no mystery for Emily but size and proportion of this particular specimen did.

The conversation had stopped. Doris knew what was going on and took a sideways glance at Amjad. His focus was fixed, straight ahead. Both her hands were on the table. Someone had to say something.

'Does anyone want another drink?' Amjad asked

perhaps a little too loudly. Emily and Tyson ignored him. Something much more interesting was going on beneath the table. Doris muttered a quiet 'Yes please Pet' and a slightly agitated Amjad got up from the table, untangling himself awkwardly from a series of barricading timber struts and moving quickly in the direction of the bar. As he disappeared inside, Doris reflected on her situation. She had done her best. Amjad was non-responsive and looked embarrassed at the continuing innuendos involving sex rattling round the conversation. She wasn't that worried and in fact another couple of large Classic Mojito's and she wouldn't really care much what Amjad did ... or who he did it with.

The situation with Emily however was heating up a little and she knew her and the chatty Tyson would be looking for some space soon; some dark space, some quiet space where their common urgencies could be satisfied. In the back of a car, BMW or no BMW, was not Emily's style. Upright against a wall at the back of the dustbins was a definite no-no. A decision would need to be made soon. Doris could see it in her eyes. Emily was wanting to go. She was getting restless. She checked her watch. That was a bad sign.

Emily knew one of two things would have to happen next. Either she would be having some rough sex with the amiable Tyson, call me Ty' ... or she would be telling him to piss off and find another vacant depository to calm his current substantial erection.

She made eye contact with Doris who shook her head slightly. Getting down and dirty with Amjad was not part of her plan that morning. A bell rang; a muffled noise from inside Geogio's. That indicated last ... very last orders. The bar had served drinks nearly twenty minutes past their standard closing time but now the manager wanted everybody outside and the door closed by three.

Emily gave Tyson the hard stare in an attempt to assess his commitment, her hand now removed from the exploratory search of his trousers. Perhaps Tyson would not be prepared to take up what was on offer, but his look confirmed there was little doubt he was definitely up for it. There would be no coded language of agreement; no more wordplay in an attempt to convey a message that had already been received. Emily was eager to get at it. There was an urgency now; one that hadn't been there earlier. A minute passed. Perhaps they were both chewing over the same dilemma.

'Whatever ye' thinkin' Pet ... A'hm not doin' it in the back o' a bloody car like ... so ye'd better get organised quick ... the rest o' the girls'll be here in a minute. The damn bar's closin' right now!'

Tyson gave out a questioning look to Amjad who nodded his head. Emily caught it.

'Something was possibly going on between these two!' she thought to herself. However, to be honest, peering through a haze of alcoholic euphoria and now feeling horny as hell, all she didn't need right now was for Nell and the rest of the girls to come steaming out of the bar and put a stop to everything.

Tyrone stood and grabbed Emily by the hand. The growth in his trousers had become embarrassingly obvious. Doris simply had to make a comment.

'A'h hope that thing in there don't spring up and choke ye when ye' drop ye' kecks like. It looks a bit restless from here Pet'

Emily laughed, taken with the moment. Something was about to happen. Tyson was in a hurry.

'Come wi' me lass' he urged guiding her away from the table and up to a door at the side of Georgio's.

'Ye'd better bring ye' handbag like!'

'Aye ... an' ye'd better bring ye' damn wallet pet wi' som'at more in it than money' countered Emily.

Tyson fumbled in his pocket for a key. It fitted the security door to one of the blocks of flats, a door which opened with a buzzing noise.

Emily knew what it was.

'A'hm not bloody well doin' it in the soddin' drafty stairwell o' a block o' flats either' she confirmed to an eager Tyson.

'No need Em. Me and Amjad ... we've got a flat here on the first floor like ... an a nice comfy bed fe' ye' te' bounce up an' down on Pet ... so let's bloody well go!'

Chapter Twenty Two
3.00 am

The door to apartment 101 opened into a small corridor. Tyson switched on a light. There was a smell of fresh paint. The corridor looked clean with several doors leading off it; the floor covering a dark grey industrial carpet that appeared recently fitted. Emily had heard about the apartments above the venues at the Marina, but had never been inside one. This was a first.

'No, put that light out Pet' Emily ordered firmly.

Putting on a light could lead to a thought that Tyson might like to show her around his small but comfortable abode, which could then lead to an offer of a drink possibly ending up with him telling her his damn life story.

She had been there before.

That was not what she was here for today.

'A'h thought ye' said ye' had a flat up on the headland like?' Emily questioned.

'Aye, I did ... but me an' Amjad, we always say that. If we're out an' meet up wi' a gang an' they knew we had a flat here, they'd all be wantin' to use it ... it'd be a bloody mess like ... condoms floor te' ceilin' Pet. So, we don't tell nobody'

'Well ... that's bloody good thinkin' Batman; so now that particular discussion is over with ... ye'd better get em' off like!'

'What ... here?'

'Aye lad ... right here ... and right now'

Tyson looked confused for a second or two.

'What ... ye' mean standin' up like?'

'Aye ... A'h mean standin' up'

The conversation was doing it for Emily, being aware of a discernable dampness between her legs brought on by heightened anticipation.

'Don't ye worry about access Pet ... A'hve got me black silky crotchless knickers on te'night. All ye've got te' do is put it in me hand. D'ya think ye' can do that Pet?'

Tyson appeared confused, making no particular attempt to take his trousers off. This had not happened to him before. He was used to being in charge ... but not tonight. The situation had grown slightly confusing but at the same time undoubtedly exhilarating. It felt as if he were somehow hovering above two people desperate for a physical connection and them not knowing he was there; a voyeuristic experience heightening his passion for the beautiful woman trapping him in the corridor and giving out instructions.

She pushed toward him, their mouths meeting in a feverish connection, tongues going wild and temperatures rising, out of control. He was back down on earth. It would be too late to go into reverse now.

Emily was on fire, pressing up against Tyson's growing bulge, feeling feverishly for the belt on his trousers, eager fingers releasing the buckle and then the zip. A pull on the underpants would release the stiffening muscle.

'Disappointing in girth ... but more than made up for in length' Emily muttered to herself. The sweating young man was silent but breathless, clumsily searching for her mouth once more. Emily knew she was now in control as she crushed her lips down on his, a tongue leaping out at her. His muscle felt hard and wild, completely uncontrolled as she pulled and caressed him in both hands, urging it to finally stiffen as he attempted to pull her awkwardly toward him.

Tyson was indeed comfortingly long, sporting several very firm inches and as was the case with the long ones, she felt it turn to a welcome, slightly bulbous shape at the end, his foreskin pulling tight over it, stretching down beneath the rim of the bulge, making it feel even larger in her hand.

She played with it, teasing it, resisting him as he pushed up against her, rhythmically and demanding like a young over excited bull on his first sexual encounter. He wanted it inside her, rough sex, no foreplay; he needed the physical release, unable to control the basic animal instinct of simply wanting to get this female impregnated.

She leaned back; stopped massaging the throbbing, extended, straining member, quickly recovering her handbag from the floor, searching and finding the necessary condom with one hand and slipping it over the glorius erection with practiced expertise. She could wait no longer. She pushed up against him once more, hard and unforgiving, bending her knees slightly with legs apart, wet and waiting to be filled.

'Put it in, for God's sake, put it in ... now!'

It was not a request, it was a command. Tyson pushed up hard with a groan of satisfaction as he felt his fully sheathed and lubricated length slip easily into her.

'Oh, Christ ... that's right good Ty' she sighed 'Not too quickly Pet, A'h want to feel ye' all the way'

The penetrating movement started slow and rhythmic at first, without urgency as she adjusted her height over him, growing to be quicker and harder as he moved deeper inside her with every push. His hands grabbed the firm, tightened muscles of her buttocks, squeezing and lifting apart. He rode her quickly, impatiently, literally shuddering with expectation. Emily was to quickly discover that Tyson was not practiced; he could control his desperation no longer climaxing with a shout, a cry of release, of physical satisfaction as he called out her name through tight lips.

It was far too quick. She needed much more. Bearing down on him, Emily felt the bulbous, latex encapsulated head pulsate and fill, the heat growing quickly inside her; it may be just enough.

'Don't stop ... Tyson don't ye' damned well stop ... Ah'm not there Pet ... A'hm not bloody well there ...!'

But then, in a further painfully long second, she was.

It came bursting upon her. Rippling delight; her whole body vibrating with the explosion and indescribable feeling of gratification combined with a desperately needed physical relief. The softening plug remained inside her, keeping her juices from covering him.

Was this was real sex? No, but right now, this was what she needed. This is what this young, smooth-skinned, inexperienced, suitably-endowed male had given her. She whispered words to him, pulling his face to hers, kissing him and circulating her hips gently, pushing down on the gradually deflating organ; squirming in an attempt to keep her still pumped lips locked around it.

Both were near to gasping when it ended, leaving them sweating with the recent exertion.

'Ah've never done it standin' up before' he said breathlessly.

'Well, ye' damned well have now' Emily offered back as she kissed him on the mouth once again. Was he ready for some more? If she got down on him, would he respond? Could there be a repeat performance in the offing? Emily gave it only a second's thought.

It was time to clean up and get out of there. Tyson put his hand down on her, feeling her hot wetness, her leakage as he gently caressed the sticky, tangled pubic hair covering her prominent mound, pushing one finger and then two inside her. If she was not careful, she knew she would have to have him again. Pulling his dampened hand up to her face, she licked it seductively before pushing the fingers gently into his mouth, letting him suck on them, tasting her juices, smelling her odour, giving him a sensual memory of this slightly desperate but singularly beautiful encounter.

Emily leaned back against the wall.

'A'h need a bathroom' she said breathlessly.

'It's the door next te' me' he confirmed.

After taking several minutes to sort herself out Emily exited the bathroom, clean and fresh, repaired makeup and looking particularly bright eyed after her rushed but generally satisfying encounter with a co-operative and eager Tyson.

'Your turn next!' she advised her grinning lover.

He touched her breasts as he moved past her in the narrow corridor; the electricity was still there. Was this an indication he wanted more?

When he finished in the bathroom the two of them stood close together, bodies touching but silent. Would he now take control? Would he grab her and push her hard down onto his bed; rip underwear from a damp panting body waiting in shuddering anticipation of a push, the rough hard push of a firm appendage deep inside her ... and then a fearsome, rhythmic movement that would go on forever and ever ... just like Justin Beiber?'

He leant forward and cupped her face in both hands, kissing her gently on the lips. Emily knew that kiss meant something from Tyson but she also knew it would not herald the beginning of anything else. This would be the end of it. There would be no more sex for Emily tonight ... unless of course Justin was in good form later.

'Time te' go?' questioned Tyson.

There were to be no complements tonight; no 'that was really good' or 'I enjoyed being inside ye' ... can we do it again sometime?' ... just the simply obvious question: 'Time te' go?'

'Yes Ty ... it's probably time te' go Pet'

With handbag firmly in hand she followed her young man out the flat, down the stairs and onto the pavement. It appeared that just about every eye, belonging to every person, now finishing their drinks sitting at the scattered timber benches, was focused only on them. That may not have been the case of course but it certainly was for one particular table occupied by six inebriated young ladies surrounding a rather beleaguered looking Amjad.

The shouts, some phrasing proposals of congratulations and others floating several theories as to what had gone on between the smiling couple, came loud and embarrassingly descriptive. Tyson looked uncomfortable and let go of Emily's hand. The table was covered in half consumed drinks and

Emily picked up the nearest one, not knowing and not particularly caring what was in it.

'We've bin thrown out Em. They won't serve any more drinks like. So, we're al' gannin yem like. There's a taxi on it's way an A'h've told em ye'll want te' go ... wi' us like ... have A'h told em right Pet?'

'Aye Nell, ye've told em right'

'Oh that's good Em ... we al' thought yous' two ... ye'd bin off te' get some fish an' chips like!'

'What made ye think that Nell' asked a curious Emily.

''Cause A'h can still see the batter runnin' down ye' leg Pet!' At this, the whole group burst into laughter except Tyson and Amjad; Tyson because he saw nothing to laugh at, therefore feeling slightly embarrassed and Amjad because he simply didn't get it.

'Well, there were no chance of fish an' chips fe' me te'night like ... isn't that right Amjad?' Doris added.

Now it was Tyson's turn to laugh.

'Oh' don't ye worry like, he' a bit of a dark horse is our Amjad but he's the kind that likes te' snuggle up on a rug in front of a roarin' fire. Isn't that right Amjad?'

'Not in the middle o' summer ye' big pillock' threw in Kylie Brooks as the seven seat taxi pulled up to the kerb, the driver tapping his horn, eager to get away on his last drop of the morning.

Chapter Twenty Three
4.00 am

The girls all piled into the taxi, a tight squeeze with six in the back and Janice Potter, the most likely to be sick, volunteered by the rest to sit in front, with the driver.

'So ... what's ye' name like?' she asked him coquettishly'

'Hussein' he replied abruptly, not wanting to engage in conversation with a bunch of drunken women.

'De' ye' know where weez' al' goin' pet?'

Hussein ran off a list of locations with Emily and Nell last, being out of town and the furthest away.

'Gi' that man a kipper Jan ...' shouted Doris Blackwell. As far as she could remember in her current state, all locations were correct.

'Now let's al' hope that none of us throws up like ... in ye' taxi afore we get home Hussein ...'

Grim faced, Hussein ignored the possible warning, concentrating on moving as quickly as the speed limits would allow on roads carrying minimum early morning traffic. He wanted to get home and not have to spend an hour when he got there cleaning sick from his nearly new Mercedes people carrier. At least the last fare of the shift would be a good one assuming they all had money on them of course.

Hussein liked cash rather than the regularly proposed alternative of a quick feel and a possible blow job in the back. He had installed concealed video units recording what went on inside and outside the vehicle, a necessary aid for any taxi driver daring to do the night shift anywhere in his particular patch.

'So Em?' questioned Nell through a smile: 'Spill the bloody beans. What were he like ... like?'

'What de' ye' mean Nell?' replied an innocent looking Emily.

The girls all sniggered in unison, prompting Janice to throw in: 'Oh ye' know pet; what happened wi' the lad wi' tight strides like. You two disappeared an' A'h saw ye' come out o' the flats Em. How de' ye' get in there Pet. Don't ye' need a bloody key or somethin'?'

'Aye' offered Doris: 'Not only did he have a key to a bloody flat on the marina like, he also had a key to a right canny BWM as well ... isn't that right Em?'

'It is' confirmed a tight lipped Emily Macklam.

'Howay hinny, ye' have te' tell us what happened like ... else we'll get Nell's marra at the Jolly Sailor te' ban ye' for a month!'

More giggling.

'He looked a bit hacky te' me like' offered Doris, determined to cause trouble.

'Well, A'h can assure ye' Doris, he were as clean as a bucket o' Daz like an' A'h gave him a right good deek an' a fair nose first Pet'

'So, can we get te' the bloody point Em ... did ye' screw 'im ... or not?'

'Divvin' be se' nebby Nell ... A'hm keepin' this te' mesel' like ... in case A'h see him again'

The girls fell silent. It looked as if Emily would not be 'coming forth' and so that would be the end of it; a disappointment indeed. However, two minutes later Emily offered out her most tantalizing smile.

'Aw ... go on then ... A'h was only teasin' ye' like ... here's how it happened!'

The girls all bent forward with a shout from Janice

in the front to 'Bloody speak up Em ... A'h don't wanna' miss a word!'

'Well' began Emily: 'A'h were quite surprised like when he dragged me up te' the door o' the flats and produced a bloody key. Him and Amjad shared a two bed an although A'h did' ne' see much of it like, it looked OK te' me'

'What were the bed like Em ...'

'A'h don't know. We didn't get any further than the damn corridor'

'The corridor?' queried a disbelieving Nell.

'Aye. A'h could ne' wait for all that damn buggerin' about like ... ye know ... the 'would ye like drink?' bit an' shall A'h show ye' me bedroom Pet?' ... so I told im' te' get on wi' it like ... and A'h had no choice but te' do him standing up!'

'Ooh ...' cried Janice: 'that were brave of ye' Pet, but bloody messy like!'

'Well, the one eyed trouser snake he had on offer were more than up te' the job ... and ye need a long one when ye's standin' up'

Six heads all nodded in agreement.

'Unfortunately girls, the first couple o' shoves set im' off an' I tried to hold him back ... but he shot his load and I had to hold him captured, pushed hard against the wall until I got some damn relief like'

'Well ye' got a shag wi'out brusies te'night Em and that's more than any of us can say' offered Nell with all heads nodding once again in complete agreement.

'A'h think yous' two should've taken up the offer from Helmut wi' the helmet an' done the three in a bed thing. De' ye think he could have handled two like ... ye' know done ye' proper like ... or maybe he had some o' them vibrators an' handcuffs ... them German's love that kind o' thing ... don't they Nell?'

offered a straight-faced Jeanie Stigwell.

'Well, that were the best thing about the bloody Common Market ladies ... it made sex aids cheaper an' more affordable for the workin' girl'

'Aye, they must a' bin costin' ye' a fortune in batteries Nell!'

More laughter!

Hussein grimaced. Not long to the first drop off.

'A'h hope ye slapped a johnnie on im' Em' someone shouted.

'Oh ... A'h did that. A'hm not stupid ladies. In fact A'h have it in me handbag here ... de' ye' girls want te' see it like ... see how much he filled it?'

Shouts of horror went up from the girls, filling the taxi with screams of laughter and Hussein praying his ordeal would be over soon.

'Anyway ... A'h have a better form of contraception than that don't ye' know. If A'h see a nice, fit lookin' fella like, an' the old juices start flowing a little bit, I think o' that bloody asshole Peter Lewis, then everything goes inta' shutdown an' the lock on me chastity belt snaps shut'

'One o' these days, the southern twat is gonna' get a bit o' a thrashin' like round the back o' that bloody hardware store ... an' Ah'm pretty sure it's gonna' hurt like!' confirmed Kylie Brooks.

The taxi went silent.

A minute or so later, with their share of the Taxi fare resting with Nell, Doris and Kylie would be the first to be offloaded.

'Night all' they shouted, standing a little wobbly on the pavement.

'Night yous two ... will ring yeez te'morra like' shouted Nell.

Hussein steered the Mercedes away from the kerb, two more drops to make and then he could go home. His passengers were now thankfully much quieter.

'Well, the night turned out al'right girls. We had a bit o' a laugh didn't we?' questioned Nell.

'Aye, an' Em had a shag ... not that Ah'm jealous o' course but it happens every damn time. Why don't we get a shag every Friday night ... it would gi' us something extra te' look forward te' like!' Janice queried.

The four remaining girls smiled.

'If you looked like Em our Janice, ye'd have em' fallin' at ye' feet Pet so be grateful fe' small mercies ... caus' if that were to happen, wi' your bloody eyesight, ye'd be constantly tripping over!' countered Nell.

Even Hussein smiled at that one.

'What's it like havin' men fallin' at ye' feet Em. What's it really like?'

'Well Janice, ye' have te' have bloody good eyesight te tell the good fe' the bad ... an' a good sense o' feel like, ye' know, when ye' feelin a trousered sausage pushing up against ye' on the dance floor ... ye have te' be able to picture what it'd be like ... when released ... an' free like ... wavin' about in its full glory an' needin' a firm hand te control it ...'

Janice would need some time to digest that one and fell silent. It would be her stop next, along with Jeanie and Pat.

With shouts of goodbye and promises to 'ring ye tomorra' the three girls were offloaded at the end of Petersfield Avenue leaving only Nell and Emily in the back of Hussein's Mercedes. The right money for all the fares had been collected and handed to the smiling driver. No one had been sick in his vehicle;

the right fare money was sitting comfortably in his jacket pocket and so far no one had offered him a blow job. Hussein's busy Friday night and now Saturday morning would shortly be at an end, as it would for both Nellie Curtis and Emily Macklam.

The two now very tired remaining passengers could only carry on a fairly stilted conversation. The night had been a good one as far as they were both concerned, but not a memorable one. Emily had managed to grab herself some reasonably satisfying sex and Nell had further enhanced her reputation in town as being a person not to mess with. Throughout the night's events conversation between Emily and Nell had often drifted to the subject of Emily's leaving and the possibility of Nell joining her. The seed of the idea was definitely there but as far as Nell was concerned, that's all it was ... a seed.

'What'll ye be gannin' yem te' Nell?' Emily asked idly.

'I'll be going te' bed wi' nothin' on but me disappointment at not connectin' wi' some well hung bull just out lookin' for someone te' practice wi' like. What about you?'

'Well, A'h never know what te' expect; whether me brother'll be home or not; what kind of bloody stink is goin' te greet me dependin' what state me Ma's in an even if the damn front door'll be wide open or not. If A'h did'ne have me Friday night out wi' you lot ... A'h think A'hd go bloody mad Nell ... totally bloody mad!'

'Well, you look after ye damn sel' and ring me in the mornin'. A'h have te' go in'te town t'morra like ... and if ye want te' come wi' me ye'd be most welcome Pet'

It was Nell's stop.

A quick kiss on the cheek and then she was gone.

Suddenly, Emily felt strangely alone. Hussein remained quiet and totally relieved that his next stop would be his last one and the circuitous journey had been completed without incident.

The anti-climax surrounded her, engulfed her even. Was she expecting too much from her life perhaps; a dissatisfied over ambitious northern girl, someone who should be satisfied with her damn lot? A tear formed; an unwelcome tear. Was it the booze or simply a welling emotion? Perhaps it was a sign from somewhere else urging her not to leave the Taxi, just stay in it forever, on a journey to God knows where ... but any damn place other than where she was now heading.

The tear fell. She wanted to get rid of it. She had no need of it. She would face the rest of the day with the same determination and emotional strength she always did ... but not for much longer!

Hussein had only one more drop and then he would be heading home.

Chapter Twenty Four
5.00 am

The front door looked shut, but close inspection would reveal it was unlocked and ajar. As Emily pushed it fully open the smell hit her. It was the unwelcome stink of sick, cheap whiskey, cigarettes and brown ale. She paused before crossing the threshold taking in a gulp of fresh air to clear her mind a fraction. The house was in complete darkness, meaning anyone could be lurking behind a door or in a room somewhere waiting to pounce; a robber, a sex predator or one of her mother's alcoholic mates.

She took her faithful folding pen-knife from her handbag. It wasn't much, but rammed home with determination it would make any individual attacker think twice before laying into her. Emily had only needed to use it once against one of her mother's so called friends and it caused a satisfyingly obvious amount of damage. The offender had never returned.

Emily switched on the light in the hall as she gently closed and locked the front door, knife in one hand and handbag in the other. She moved through the house, switching on lights as she went, checking every room. Her brother must still be in the cells, getting himself ready for an early morning breakfast she thought, as he certainly wasn't at home. Her mother lay across her bed semi naked, emitting a sonorous snoring and snorting, successfully imitating the sounds of a fully contented sow.

The unacceptable smell came from the kitchen. Someone had been violently sick. The table creaked under the load of empty bottles and cans. Emily, switching on the extract fan, considered tackling the mess of drying sick and then thought better of it. That could wait; her need to catch up on some sleep could not. She checked the clock on the kitchen wall; a few minutes past five. She climbed the stairs, her growing sadness weighing her down. Entering her bedroom, her one place of sanity, she hurriedly locked the door and threw herself on the bed.

After several minutes of just laying there, perhaps looking for inspiration ... but 'inspiration' for what, Emily raised herself; dress off first, then makeup, then a pee. The motions were mechanical, robotic even and minutes later she was back, between the sheets and looking for just an hour or two's peace before having to rise up again; face the sick on the kitchen floor, lever her mother into an upright position and field the constant nagging questions from the policewoman and social worker who would no doubt arrive at some time during the morning with her brother.

She closed her eyes, her hands feeling the satisfying flatness of her stomach, prepared and eager to co-operate with any instructions provided by Justin Bieber ... should he take time from his busy schedule to visit her again. She should have showered, discarded her soiled underwear and gotten the smell of Tyson away from her. She knew that of course, but right now she was glad of it; glad of the smell of a man tucked up tight in bed with her, a strong male odour, one that made her smile rather than the sweet all pervading aroma of human sickness that inhabited every nook and cranny of this damnable dwelling.

She shut her eyes tight, hoping to peer into the blackness behind them to picture a better future for herself than ... this! The burden of carrying her mother and brother had become too damn difficult to handle. There was little or no help available to someone like Emily. She had rung all the bloody useless child lines when she was younger. She had sat for hours in the offices of various social services operators from councils and charities since she became a teenager. These angels of love and understanding had mostly offered to do nothing about her situation other than put her in care when she was younger and send her on an anger management course when they ran out of other agencies to shift her over to.

Emily knew the plusses and the minuses of her situation. Her brother, or half brother as she used to remind the various policemen and women who invaded her life with monotonous regularity, was a matter considered by her to be out of control. He needed a father. Even more than that, he needed a father who would give him a damn good clip round the ear. However, that was not about to happen, so all the wishful thinking in the world would not save Thomas Macklam ... he was a lost cause.

Her mother was a sick person who needed treatment. She needed time in any sort of establishment that would force her to dry out, push her through withdrawal and build her up again physically. She needed psychiatric care to dig out from her dulling mind the rotting bones of a husband she nursed through months of what most recognised as a painful and distressing death. Then the guilt she had carried for so long, cheating on her sick husband as he lay generally breathless and unable to move from his favourite chair in his beloved conservatory. The arrival of Thomas had eventually sent her over the edge. Eventually her drinking would stop her working; her debts would force the family home to be sold and her responsibilities would necessarily have to be picked up more and more by a young, struggling Emily.

Her eyes dampened; the uninvited emotion building. She squeezed them tighter shut. It wasn't any form of pity for herself causing the ache in the pit of her stomach, but her mother; someone she would be leaving soon; leaving to simply fall off the edge. Her new life in London would provide little or no room for feelings of guilt, pity, sorrow or any other emotion focusing on the negative. She had spent nearly all her life doing that; becoming physically and emotionally weary to the point of exhaustion on a near daily basis.

Were there fun times as well? Did her mother take her and her brother to the seaside for example and perhaps add to the excitement of the day with a delicious, cooling ice cream or sticky candy floss? No ... was the answer! If there were such good times, then Emily had either forgotten them or buried them so far in the back of her mind they were totally irretrievable.

The tears eventually came. She tried hard to stop them, but the weariness eventually overtook her. Then came the sobs; indications she really had had enough. She had money saved; in the bank where her thieving mother could not get her hands on it. The weekend after next her and Nell were going to take a 'sickey' at work for a couple of days and go down to London, check out the work opportunities and the cost of finding Emily some form of acceptable accommodation. If it was somehow bad news she would handle it; she had been handling bad news for most of her life. However, Emily had grit and determination and she had been convinced by Nell and others that was all she needed to 'get on' in a place like London. She would not be deterred, not put off on her quest for a better life and one without the millstones of a drunken mother and delinquent brother weighing heavily round her neck.

It was time to get some rest. She had been on what would be scored in her daily diary as a nine out of ten night, with the result pushed up the scoreboard by some great exchanges with the girls and of course the unbelievably satisfying stand up event with Tyrone; an encounter which was spontaneous, a little bit risky and very erotic.

With tears now dried, emotions under control and more pleasing images filling the blackness behind sleeping eyes, Emily's face took on a contented smile. There really were some good things to cherish in what was a particularly hard life for Emily Macklam and there would no doubt be good memories to reflect upon in London of life, her life, in the North East ... as a northern girl.

Justin Bieber had agreed to get his kit off. This time he meant it. He had whispered it to her. He stood in front of her as he had done many times before, the image appearing closer and closer in the emerging vision; the top half of a shimmering, sweat laden muscular and tanned torso now in temptingly full focus with other previously blurred and distant features gradually clearing. Emily reached out. She wanted to bring him nearer, smell him, touch him, make sure it really was him in the flesh, sure he would not suddenly disappear or move out of reach.

A pair of smooth skinned, finely developed and unblemished masculine hands dropped to waist level, beginning to tug suggestively at the belt on a pair of stone washed and fashionably threadbare jeans. She had been here before. She waited expectantly for some form of unwelcome intrusion attempting to blank out her pleasurable thoughts and force the image of one tantalisingly fit looking Justin to retreat back into distant darkness. She would beg, she would wish, she would shed real tears if necessary.

Justin continued manipulating the top band of his jeans, free from the restrictive binding of the wide leather belt. His hand felt down inside; her hands moved with him, down beneath the clinging sheets to feel eagerly between dampening thighs. He was talking to her, but she couldn't understand what he was saying. She shouted out. He continued to take a step nearer, his hand moving invitingly inside his half zipped jeans. It was too much for Emily. She could not wait for him ... No, she would not wait for him ... and then it came upon her; a shuddering body, a near spiritual internal warmth spreading over her, a massive feeling of relief and an expectation that this may be followed by another.

Justin Bieber had played his part. It didn't happen often like that, but when it did it was worth a hundred fumbling, pushing and sweating Tyrone's and now what she needed most was rest ... long peaceful rest, charging her depleted batteries to prepare for yet another day at the coal face of her particular and unique life experiences; the life of one Emily Macklam ... a northern girl!

THE END

Copyright © 2019 Quentin Cope

www.quentincope.co.uk

48820768R00116

Printed in Poland
by Amazon Fulfillment
Poland Sp. z o.o., Wrocław